# WHAT CHILD IS THIS?

'What Child is this, who laid to rest
  On Mary's lap is sleeping?
Whom angels greet with anthems sweet
  While shepherds watch are keeping?'
            —William Chatterton Dix (1837–1898)

Also by Bonnie MacBird

*Art in the Blood*
*Unquiet Spirits*
*The Devil's Due*
*The Three Locks*

# What Child is This?

## A SHERLOCK HOLMES
## CHRISTMAS ADVENTURE

### BONNIE MacBIRD

WITH ILLUSTRATIONS BY
FRANK CHO

COLLINS
CRIME
CLUB

This book is a new and original work of fiction featuring Sherlock Holmes,
Dr Watson, and other fictional characters that were first introduced to the world in
1887 by Sir Arthur Conan Doyle, all of which are now in the public domain. The
characters are used by the author solely for the purpose of story-telling and not
as trademarks. This book is independently authored and published and is
not sponsored or endorsed by, or associated in any way with, Conan Doyle
Estate, Ltd. or any other party claiming trademark rights in any of
the characters in the Sherlock Holmes canon.

**COLLINS CRIME CLUB**

An imprint of HarperCollins*Publishers*
1 London Bridge Street
London SE1 9GF

www.harpercollins.co.uk

HarperCollins*Publishers*
1st Floor, Watermarque Building, Ringsend Road
Dublin 4, Ireland

Published by Collins Crime Club 2022
1

Illustrations © Frank Cho 2022
Drop Cap design © Mark Mázers 2022

Bonnie MacBird asserts the moral right
to be identified as the author of this work.

A catalogue record for this book is available from the British Library

Hardcover: 978-0-00-852128-8
Trade Paperback: 978-0-00-852131-8

Set in Sabon by Palimpsest Book Production Ltd, Falkirk, Stirlingshire

Printed and bound in the UK using 100% Renewable Electricity
by CPI Group (UK) Ltd

MIX
Paper | Supporting
responsible forestry
FSC
www.fsc.org
FSC™ C007454

This book is produced from independently certified FSC™ paper
to ensure responsible forest management.

For more information visit: www.harpercollins.co.uk/green

# Contents

## PART FOUR – THE NEWBORN KING

## PART FIVE – PEACE ON EARTH

*For Kirstin Kay*

'O Tannenbaum, o Tannenbaum!
Dein Kleid will mich was lehren . . .'

*'O Christmas Tree, O Christmas Tree!*
*Your needles want to teach me something . . .'*
—German Christmas song loved by Prince Albert,
Queen Victoria's husband

# *Prologue*

ondon snow is rare in the early twenty-first century, but one evening in late December of 2021 some tentative flakes drifted lazily down outside the window of my small mansion flat just off Baker Street. A miniature Christmas tree sat in one corner of my study, lights twinkling, adding a touch of festivity to the place.

I have often wondered at the history of the room in which I now sat. The building was new in 1890 and its residents have roamed the halls during the Victorian and Edwardian eras, both World Wars, the Swinging Sixties and now the pandemic era. Sometimes, late at night, a small animation plays through my imagination. The furniture shifts places and changes shapes, the walls dissolve into different colours, and the shadows of past residents move about, eating and sleeping, arguing, laughing, enduring, mourning, celebrating and living their daily lives through more than one hundred and thirty years.

Old buildings such as this are filled with ghosts. Perhaps even my own lingering spirit will someday echo to a future resident. But on a certain chilly, late December day in 2021 all these faded, for I had come upon an unexpected Christmas treat—and a direct link to the past.

Some years ago, after the publication of a previously undiscovered John Watson manuscript about his friend Sherlock Holmes, which I had discovered in the Wellcome Library, a mysterious woman named Lydia gave me a large box filled with other treasures. And on this chilly December evening I found, to my surprise, tucked inside a larger notebook, a smaller schoolboy notebook with a worn, dark green cover.

In it, written in faded green ink, a long-past London holiday season came to life. It was an undated Sherlock Holmes Christmas tale told by John Watson.

It has never before been made public.

Of course, I was familiar with his previously discovered Christmas bonbon, *The Blue Carbuncle*. But not this. Watson had originally titled this story O *Tannenbaum*, but then crossed this out. Instead, he had settled on *What Child is This?*

I opened the pages and read. To my surprise, frozen in time, was a remarkable view of a long-ago Christmas, showing a new facet of Sherlock Holmes. Just as Watson once found in Holmes's handshake 'a strength for which I should hardly have given him credit', here the good doctor revealed in Holmes a sensitivity we might not expect.

Let me leave you with one more wintry London image. Earlier in the day, I had been out for a walk in Regent's Park before the weather turned and had been surprised by some very late-season, pale pink roses in Queen Mary's Gardens. The roses were in full bloom and yet encased in a glistening, silvery coat of frost.

I had never seen a frozen rose before. Who would have guessed that in late December, these delicate blossoms would live on, enrobed in ice?

But in London at Christmastime, I suppose, anything is possible. Enjoy, then, this sparkling winter rose—John Watson's recounting of *What Child is This?*

—Bonnie MacBird
London, December 2021

# PART ONE

## HARK THE HERALD

*'Hope is the pillar that holds up the world.*
*Hope is the dream of a waking man.'*
—Pliny the Elder (AD 23–79)

# CHAPTER 1

## *Joy to the World*

‘lose the window, would you, Watson? Those infernal Christmas Carols are enough to drive one mad.’

It was the morning of the thirteenth of December, two days into my extended visit to 221B, and to my irritable friend Sherlock Holmes the relentless cheer of the holiday season threatened to wash over Baker Street like an unwelcome tide of effluvia.

Today, despite the winter chill, I had cracked open the windows to let out the rank odour of a chemistry experiment with which Holmes amused himself in a corner of the sitting-room. At that very moment the haunting melody of 'We Three Kings' floated up from the street below. The silvery children's voices were a treat to my ears, but clearly not to my unsentimental companion.

As it had every Christmastime during my residence with Holmes, the sombre, subdued atmosphere of our old sitting-room—with nary a pine bough nor a sprig of mistletoe in sight—was in sharp contrast to the sparkling streets of London with all its lights, decorated shop windows, music and excited children.

I closed the window with a sharp bang. 'Done. Now, then, if you would please cease your malodorous experiments, Holmes. Have a little consideration, would you?' Something sulphurous and ghastly continued to permeate the close air. It was barely ten in the morning.

He sighed theatrically and leaned back in his chair. 'As you wish, Watson.'

I had begun to regret offering to spend some days before Christmas with my friend, but Mary had felt obliged to assist a recently widowed acquaintance of hers for a few days in Chester. She had encouraged me to visit Sherlock Holmes, whom she suspected was in need of some holiday cheer.

This was unlikely, I thought, knowing my friend's dislike of what he called the 'enforced jollity' of the season. But perhaps an intriguing case would offer both of us a needed distraction. What ensued in this memorable Christmas season proved far more than that.

Holmes once said of his nemesis Moriarty that the man was at the centre of a spider's web, with a thousand radiations into the criminal underworld. But as I was about to discover, my friend's ability to casually extend his own network of helpers throughout the city was perhaps greater.

And it was during this case that this magnetism was most illuminated to me, as he almost effortlessly attracted a constellation of London's secret angels in order to champion the downtrodden.

Holmes turned off his Bunsen burner and was now furiously writing notes about whatever had been bubbling back there. The purpose of his tinkering, and of the boiling and sizzling and clinking going on in the corner of that room, was a puzzle.

I was grateful he had extinguished the flame. Damage from any small explosions or fires would be devilishly difficult to have repaired just now, as most craftsmen who could afford a holiday were off celebrating the season.

And many of the rest were no doubt engaged in repairs following the various household conflagrations caused by the folly of candlelit Christmas trees. Those, I knew, were inspired by the late Prince Albert and his enthusiasm for the Germanic Christmas traditions of his childhood.

My own golden memories of my time with Holmes centred not at all around such homely traditions, but entirely on the excitement of our many cases. I had cast from my mind the number of times his chemical explorations had sent me running madly to the nearest public house, where a smoke-filled room offered air fresher than did our own abode. How selective are our recollections!

To distract myself just then, I cracked open the thick book on my lap. I had once mentioned a desire to patch up holes in my classical education, and two years ago Holmes had given me this at Christmas: *The Natural History of Pliny*. I hoped that for once I would make it through the first chapter without falling asleep.

'How are you doing with Pliny?' inquired Holmes with a slightly malicious grin.

'You know, of course, how he died?' I asked.

Holmes looked up from his notebook.

I waved my hand in the air to dispel the fumes. 'Died from inhaling poisonous gases,' I said.

'Ha, ha, Watson, *touché*!' said he. 'Yes, Pliny succumbed to poisonous gases when he went to make a scientific study of the recent eruption of Mount Vesuvius.'

'I thought his purpose was to rescue people in Pompeii,' said I.

'Have it your way, Watson. But point taken. Now, let me continue my calculations here.'

The doorbell rang below us. A case, perhaps? Oh, blessed relief!

But I was disappointed when a young woman of our acquaintance burst onto the landing. It was Miss Hephzibah O'Malley, whom I had met earlier on a case I had written up as *The Devil's Due*. Despite her small stature and rough East End exterior, 'Heffie', as we called her, had proven to be a formidable ally.

The girl was a force of nature. Seventeen years old and the orphaned daughter of an Irish prize fighter and a Jewish schoolteacher, she had grown up in the roughest part of London almost entirely on her own.

What resulted was the remarkable and highly intelligent young lady who now stood at the threshold of our sitting-room. As always, she stood out with her remarkable halo of wild blonde curls—which escaped her chignon and framed her face like the mane of a small lion—as well as for the expression of fierce concentration that gave anyone in the vicinity the distinct impression that she would brook no nonsense from them. And I knew first-hand that the diminutive girl was physically capable of bringing a much larger opponent to his knees.

Today Heffie was uncharacteristically clothed in a perfectly respectable dress of forest-green wool and a matching shawl. From the door to our sitting-room, she stared at a distracted Holmes with a penetrating force.

'Mr 'olmes?'

Holmes tore his gaze away from a pipette in his hand. He set it down in frustration. 'You have entirely destroyed my concentration,' said he.

'Mr 'olmes, I am 'ere to ask you a question,' said Heffie. Her accent, as always, was unmistakably Cockney. 'I needs some advice.'

Holmes sighed, stood up from his table and bade her sit.

'You still have your position with the police?' he asked, sitting opposite her on the divan.

Heffie, mired in poverty when I first met her, had shown herself to be brave, resourceful and a powerful force for good. Her assistance with that horrific series of London murders had been helpful beyond all expectation. Lestrade had noticed, too, and Holmes had managed to find the quick-witted girl a paid position with the Metropolitan Police.

She remained standing. 'Today I do,' she said with a grin. 'Though them's not exactly my type.'

'No one expected that they were, Heffie,' said Holmes. 'But you and Scotland Yard have a mutual goal.'

'Sure enough.' A unique position had been created for her by Lestrade, himself newly promoted. She was a kind of unofficial but paid adjunct, listed on the books as a 'resource' but in actuality serving as the police force's eyes and ears all over the city. She had proved herself invaluable. Lestrade had told us so, only last week.

She frowned. 'To the point, Mr 'olmes. I must be off,' said the girl. 'I'm movin' 'ouse again. At least I think so. 'Ere's the thing. See this dress?'

'Yes, and it's quite lovely,' I said. While plain, it was of pleasing cut and colour. It was a marked change from the dishevelled rags she had been wearing when I had first met her.

''S'the problem. Soon as I got some new clothes, people where I live looked at me different, like. It's not as if I'm parading with jewellery and all—jus' clothes for work, I 'splained. But, no matter, they got their backs up about it, and someone stole my new shoes. The villains!'

'I see you have replaced them,' I said, eyeing her well-shod feet. Sturdy brown winter boots peeked out from under her skirts. Not exactly elegant, but new and fit for purpose.

'No, I got 'em back, and the woman won't be doin' that again,' said Heffie, raising her fists with a grin. 'But, still, I moved out.'

'Good for you,' I said. 'Tell us.'

Holmes looked heavenward. Heffie turned to him with a fierce stare.

'Well, after me boots, I moved into nicer rooms, just off King's Cross, to be closer to work and all. But I needs advice 'cos they didn't like me, neither.'

Holmes stared at her in consternation. '*Either*. If you have come to me for social advice, Heffie, you might do better at your local public house.'

'Or anywhere, frankly,' I added with a grin. 'But Heffie, tell us, why do they not like you at your new place?'

'Same reason as the last place. Well, not exactly the same. My clothes match theirs, at least. But 'cos I'm working for the police.'

'I don't follow,' said I.

'It's not a respectable job to most people, Watson,' said Holmes impatiently. 'But Heffie, respect of that kind is not your concern, is it? Just ignore them and go about your work.'

'I s'pose. I 'elped catch a ring o' thieves and pickpockets only last week.'

Holmes smiled. 'The Johnston gang. Yes, Lestrade told me. Fine work, Heffie. Working the Covent Garden area, were they?'

I had read something of that. A group of young boys, trained by some latter-day Fagin, had been terrorizing the honest working men and women of that area and had recently grown violent in their tactics. One poor vegetable seller's assistant had been sent to hospital while attempting to defend his meagre earnings from the gang.

'You would think they would aim for richer purses,' said I. 'They must be desperate to target the workers there.'

'Watson,' said Holmes, 'they work there precisely because they blend in. And yes, they are desperate.'

Outside the singing children had grown louder and 'Hark the Herald Angels Sing' crept past our closed window and edged into the room. Holmes glowered at this intrusion.

'Ah, those carollers! They should all be dunked in the Thames. But why are you here, Heffie?'

The girl reached down the front of her dress to retrieve something, felt around as whatever she was trying to find had evidently slipped, and I looked away, embarrassed.

'Reticule, Heffie,' said Holmes. 'You should have a *reticule*. Ladies carry their things in—'

'*Nah!*' said Heffie. 'They grab them *ready-cools* right off you in the streets. You wouldn't know. You ain't never been a lady.' She pulled the paper out from her dress.

'Oh, yes, he has,' I laughed. Holmes had certainly gone out disguised as an old woman, at least several times to my knowledge.

Heffie handed Holmes the slip of paper. ''Ere's where the leader of the Johnston gang lives. Lestrade only got 'is main 'elper.'

'Why not give this to Lestrade?' Holmes asked. 'Or collar him yourself? You are certainly capable.'

'No, I ain't. 'E's not right in the 'ead, and I ain't going there. I'm tellin' you because Lestrade's already got a—what you call it?—commendation for this. The bloke's not willing to look no more at it.'

'Try again,' said Holmes. 'You must learn to navigate the hierarchy there.'

To my surprise, Heffie seemed to know exactly what he meant, and with a 'Cheerio!' she departed. His eyes wandered back to the chemistry table.

'Holmes, please. I don't think I can stand any more of your experiments just now. I have an errand on Oxford Street. Let us go out for some air and a sandwich.'

'I am not hungry.'

'We will enjoy the Yuletide decorations. The lights. The shop windows.'

'You are arguing against your case, Watson.'

'I insist. Or I shall go alone—but trust me, I will make you pay later.'

Holmes groaned. But somehow I managed to pry him out of 221B and into the streets. And that is where it all began.

# CHAPTER 2

## *Outrage on Oxford Street*

roast beef sandwich and two glasses of cider did wonders for my spirits, but little, I was sorry to note, for my friend. His Scrooge-like mood persisted as we made our way along Oxford Street back towards Baker Street. Throngs of gaily dressed Christmas shoppers in heavy winter coats and bright scarves impeded our progress along the pavement, and I noted my companion growing increasingly impatient. Trying for a cab was impossible. The roadway was jammed and every available vehicle was full.

The air was crisp and frosty, which for some added to the seasonal cheer. Jostled by a group of schoolchildren with shrill voices, Holmes stopped abruptly.

'Watson, I have had enough of these crowds. Come, we will take a back way.' But just as he cut through the

throng towards an alley, a woman's scream pierced the air.

At that moment all of Christmas changed.

We turned to see a beautiful, well-dressed lady clutching a small boy as a tall man in a cloak and hood tried to wrestle the child from her arms. I got a quick glimpse of his face, pale eyes contorted in a fierce frown, the rest masked by a scarf. A second woman tried vainly to beat him off.

This commotion took place in plain sight, some twenty feet from us, with people all around. Without a thought, Holmes and I pushed through the crowd towards the struggle.

Before we could reach them, the attacker had knocked down both the mother and what appeared to be an accompanying female servant. People around them screamed and backed away. The two women and the child were on the pavement, the child of perhaps four years, wild-eyed in fear. Packages were strewn around them.

The hooded man froze for an instant, then, despite the milling crowd, he reached down and succeeded in wrenching the child away.

The next seconds were critical.

'Mummy!' the boy cried.

'Call the police!' someone shouted.

That instant, Holmes and another man were on the abductor, bringing him down, with Holmes pulling the child from the man's grasp just as the villain himself tumbled to the ground.

Holmes hesitated a second, holding the stunned child, then thrust the boy at me, and I caught the little fellow. He turned back to the assailant, but the man had leapt to his feet and was pushing his way through the crowd.

Holmes followed.

'Help her!' shouted a woman.

'She's hurt!'

I turned to the mother, who was sprawled on the pavement, her beautiful velvet cloak dirtied by the fall, and her hand to her cheek, which had suffered a blow.

More exhortations came from the crowd, but little actual help was forthcoming.

The servant, next to the elegant young woman on the pavement, leaned towards her. Seeing that her mistress was mostly unhurt, the young woman arose and gently took the child from me.

'Thank you,' said she. 'Jonathan, little one! Dear God!'

Behind me, I heard distant shouts and looked but saw no sign of Holmes or the attacker through the dense crowd. If anyone could catch the man, it would be my friend. Another man who had tried to help lurched painfully up from the pavement and shrugged helplessly.

I knelt by the fallen mother and extended my hand to help her up. 'I am a doctor,' I said gently. 'Are you hurt, madam? You have had quite a shock.'

'I . . . I am unhurt,' said she.

She took my hand and rose, her face white, eyes filled with tears. Fortunately, I saw only a small scratch on her cheek, but no swelling, no bruising.

'Jonathan,' said she, taking the child from her servant. His cries had turned into keening moans which softened as she caressed his golden locks. Jonathan wrapped his arms around his mother's neck. She held the boy close, kissing the top of his head.

'There, there, darling,' said she. The maid retrieved the child's cap from the pavement and placed it on his head.

The mother looked up at me. 'Please give me your card, sir, so I may properly thank you. Can someone please call us a cab?'

I fished in my pocket for Holmes's card, which I had continued to carry with me at all times out of habit (and perhaps hope). I was aware that a small crowd had gathered around us in a tight ring, bubbling with curiosity. As was the way with the public, everyone felt obliged to weigh in on the situation.

'An outrage,' cried one.

'And at Christmastime, too!'

'The boy, is he all right?

'Can you imagine, trying to steal a child in this crowd!'

From ahead of us on the street I heard the shrill whistle of the police.

'I need to get him home,' said the mother, pulling her little boy closer.

I looked out once again for Holmes but neither he nor the attacker were visible. 'Holmes!' I called out.

I heard a shout and a police whistle again, farther in the distance, and realized the villain was perhaps still fleeing through the crowd. But what had happened to Holmes?

Though drawn to follow, I nevertheless turned back to the lady, who stood embracing her little boy, covering his tear-streaked face with kisses. His cries had subsided and he hiccoughed in the aftermath, his arms wrapped around his mother's neck. All was well.

'I have a cab for you, madam,' called out a young man, who had somehow managed to engage one despite the crowds.

The servant picked up the last of her packages with help from passers-by, now emboldened once the crisis had passed. The young man and I both helped the three into the cab.

I held out Holmes's calling card and said, 'I am Dr John Watson. My friend has gone after your attacker. His name is Sherlock Holmes, this is his card. If you would like assistance in pursuing justice, you could not do better than—'

The lady was occupied with her child, but the servant leaned out of the open door and snatched the card just before the young man who had called the cab slammed it shut. Mistaking my intentions, he said, 'Hardly the time to be soliciting business, sir!'

Ignoring him, I inquired, 'If I may have your name, madam?'

The lady glanced up. 'Thank you, Doctor, for your help. My name is—' But the cab took off and her last words were lost to me.

Irritated by this, I shot a glare at the young man, then turned back to the crowd and began making my way along the street in the direction in which the villain had fled. As if to punctuate the disturbing event, it suddenly began to snow heavily. I pulled my collar tighter and continued on. My friend then appeared, walking in my direction. I could read at once the disappointment in his posture.

Holmes arrived at my side, pale and breathing heavily. 'Slippery fellow, Watson. And resourceful. Were it not for this infernal Christmas throng, I would have had him.'

He shuddered with the cold and I pulled him inside the nearest shop, a bell tinkling as I did so. A blessed warmth surrounded us. Standing near the door, we looked out through festive pine boughs hanging above the mullioned windows to watch the snow that now came down in a deluge. The hats and shoulders of passers-by turned white. It was a veritable Christmas card if one were of artistic bent.

Holmes slowly began to catch his breath. The man must have been remarkably fit to have outrun him. 'Did no one try to assist?' I asked.

'He seized and threw two people into my path,' said he bitterly. 'Fortunately they were unharmed.' In spite of the warmth where we now stood, he shivered again.

'Some tobacco, gentlemen?' came a voice behind us, more pointed than polite. We had happened upon a smokers' emporium. The proprietor stood behind a long glass counter.

Holmes looked over at him, distracted. 'What? No.'

'Then I will kindly ask you to—'

'Have you any Havanas?' I asked, reaching for my purse.

'I do,' said the fellow, a smile lighting up his face. 'Behind me, here. How many?'

I asked the price and purchased two cigars. The shop-keeper happily rang up the sale.

'You are too polite, Watson, by half,' whispered Holmes. 'Havanas are not your favourites.'

'No, but they are yours. Merry Christmas.'

I handed Holmes his gift.

'Thank you,' he said, pocketing the cigars. 'But, *Bah humbug* anyway.'

I laughed. Sherlock Holmes, ever the curmudgeon! We pulled up our collars and rushed out into the frigid swirl of snow.

# CHAPTER 3

# A Man Missing his Ride

 n hour later, we were warm and dry in Baker Street. Holmes, now in his dressing-gown, unwrapped his cigars and sniffed one, savouring the aroma. 'Excellent choice, Watson,' said he. 'Now I must think of what might suit you.'

'No gifts are necessary,' I said, thinking that the excitement of the recent contretemps in Oxford Street was perhaps my Christmas gift in disguise. My satisfaction in helping to rescue the little boy, however, was offset by a sense of unease that the would-be abductor was still free.

I still, of course, had the damned Pliny. I was only just forcing myself to it. Holmes habitually ignored gift giving, but when feeling obligated would bestow 'improving' gifts. I, on the other hand, have always found a small, unexpected luxury to be far more pleasing to give or receive.

But these holiday musings were interrupted by the sound of the doorbell below.

Oh, how I hoped it would be a case.

Moments later, a tall, heavyset man, middle aged, with rosy cheeks and a long, thin nose shaped oddly with a ball at the tip, stared down at us with an aristocratic sneer from just inside the door. He was clad in a fitted velvet jacket, jodhpurs and tall riding boots, as though he'd just dismounted from a pleasure ride in the country. How very odd, I thought, to traipse around the city in this attire.

Perhaps even more curious, in his hand he carried a riding-crop. He tapped it impatiently against his leg.

Holmes stared at him in amusement as Mrs Hudson peeked from behind this strange figure to announce, 'The Marquis of Blandbury.' Behind his back, she gave him a disapproving look and disappeared.

'I have just been riding in the park,' proclaimed the man.

'Indeed,' said Holmes. 'And at considerable speed.'

'Speed, Holmes?' I inquired with a smile. Sometimes I feel my role is to allow, even to incite him to show off.

'The elongated, horizontal mud splatter on his boots, Watson. Nearly eradicated by the current snowfall. But not quite.' He smiled. 'Trajectory.' With a sideways glance at our visitor, Holmes picked up his pipe from a side table. 'And, of course, one might remark upon the riding-crop, which you brandish here, sir, for reasons yet to be revealed.'

His jibe missed the mark. The man simply looked down at it, as if surprised to find the whip in his own hand.

'*Hmm*, yes. Well, I do like riding fast. The faster the

better. It's frowned upon in town here, but oh, well. A country man must seek some distraction here in the city.'

'Dangerous on the ice, though,' I remarked.

'Not if one knows how to ride.'

I was thinking more of his unfortunate steed but did not voice this.

'Distraction from what? Please state your business, sir. I am very busy,' said Holmes, attending further to his pipe.

'Busy? In your dressing-gown? May I inquire what occupies you so?' The Marquis glanced around the room and frowned. He began again to tap his whip against his jodhpurs.

'Put your whip down, sir,' said Holmes. 'Unless it is your intention to hurry us along, too?'

'This? Oh, no. Well, I was speaking to my man at the stables. Apparently they are quite admiring of your skills over there. I took the decision to come sooner rather than later. *Et voilà.*'

Holmes smiled to himself and, raising an eyebrow at me, nodded subtly towards our visitor.

I stood up and took the whip from the Marquis, setting it down carefully on a table by the door. In the past we had encountered hostility, even unprovoked attacks in this very room. 'Would you care to sit down? A brandy perhaps, sir?' I asked.

'I suppose so.' The man glanced uncomfortably at his treasured possession, then taking a deep breath lowered himself onto the settee. He sat forward, fitful and edgy.

'I have come to you with a problem,' said he. 'Before all

this today, I read of your exploits and thought, well, *ho*, if anyone can find Reginald, it would be you. I was going to come to you tomorrow, but . . . my man at the stables, he used to be in my service . . . he spoke so enthusiastically . . . Well, I would like to engage you and your friend here. Doctor . . . uh, Doctor—'

'Watson,' Holmes said. 'What troubles you, sir?'

I handed the Marquis a brandy. He looked at it in confusion, as if he'd forgotten that he'd just accepted the offer. 'Oh, yes.' He set it down. 'Reginald appears to be missing,' said he.

'At last, to the point,' said Holmes. 'Who is Reginald and what are the circumstances of his being currently not in view by your august self?'

'Not in view! What an odd choice of words, considering the situation.'

I rather thought he would object to 'august self'.

'I have yet to hear what *is the situation*,' said Holmes. 'And your full name, sir.'

The man took a deep breath, leaned back on the settee and crossed his legs. His expensive, mud-splattered riding boots creaked as he did so.

'I am the Marquis of Blandbury—Henry Weathering, by name. My country seat is in the Midlands, east of Birmingham. I have three sons. Robert, Randolf, and Reginald. Fine young men. Reginald is the youngest. He is . . .' and here the man faltered. 'Well, I will admit it, Reginald is my wife's favourite. And, well, mine too.'

Holmes tsked and shifted in his chair. 'Favourite. Why?'

'Reginald, he . . . he has charm. He shows his mother great care. The boy is kind, but perhaps a little too delicate. The other two are sporting men like myself. Hunting, fishing, riding. More companionable, at least to me. And yet Reginald . . .' The Marquis trailed off, looking about.

'Pray tell us more of Reginald. In what way is he delicate?' said Holmes.

'Well, perhaps that is the wrong word.'

There was a pause.

'I cannot supply the right one until I know more. Is it his health that concerns you?' asked Holmes.

'No. Not his health. He is, he is . . . highly intelligent. Well read. Artistic. Not a sporting man. He is deeply moved by things. He will even cry at a concert or in a museum. Like a child.'

'Not like a child, Lord Blandbury. Art and music speak to the soul,' said Holmes. At the Marquis's puzzled frown, he added, 'For some.'

'Waste of emotion. I am a man of commerce, myself. My title was awarded on the basis of my industrial expertise, my charitable—'

'Let us return to Reginald. The facts, please. How old is this favoured son, this delicate, sensitive soul? How long has he been missing? Where was he last seen?'

'You mock me.'

'Not at all.'

'My son is twenty-one.'

'An adult, then.'

'More or less.'

27

'Go on.'

'What is that smell?' said the Marquis, looking around him in annoyance.

'Sulphur. Where did you see Reginald last, sir?'

'Early October. Right here! Well, not a ten-minute walk from here. Three minutes in a fast carriage.'

'What was he doing in London?'

'I bought him a flat in Mayfair, you see,' said the Marquis. 'His Christmas gift last year. He loves the theatre, the opera, and spending time in London. I set him up here.'

'To live entirely on his own?' Holmes peered at the man through a curtain of smoke.

'No. With his valet, Perkins. George Perkins. The man has been with the family for years. He is like an older brother to Reginald. I knew that he would look after my boy. Hell, he's served my Reggie since the child was only thirteen.'

'In October, what transpired between you and Reginald? Was there a dispute of some sort?'

'No. Well, perhaps I criticized his clothing.'

Holmes laughed suddenly, then caught himself. 'Sorry. Do go on.'

'He writes to his mother regularly. She rarely leaves the estate, and she lives for those letters. But they stopped more than a month ago. I have cabled Reginald several times with no reply. I am . . . I am quite worried.'

'Worried or angry?'

'Worried. And angry. Damned inconsiderate of him.'

'And then what did you do?'

'I cabled George Perkins directly. The valet replied that

all was well, and that Reginald's cable to us must have been lost. He said he'd see to my son maintaining contact.'

'When was this?'

'I don't know. Three weeks ago? I have since heard nothing.'

'It *is* the holiday season,' said Holmes, tapping his pipe on the ashtray. 'May it soon subside.'

'Yes, and Reginald is ruining my wife's Christmas.'

'Pity. But this hardly seems cause for alarm,' said Holmes.

'You have not seen the woman's tears. This is out of character for our boy. She fears the worst. And there is more. Six days ago, I asked my cousin here in London to drop by his Mayfair flat, if only to reassure me that all was well. But there was no answer there, and later my cousin learned from a maid who services several flats in the building that she had been told *not* to report to my son's any longer for cleaning.'

'Perhaps they engaged a private maid.'

The Marquis sighed and seemed lost in dark thoughts. He shook his head.

The fire spat, and I got up to turn the log.

'Do not make me work for this, my lord,' prompted my friend.

'Here is the curious thing. This maid said that there were no longer two men living there but rather a married couple now.'

'Have you gone there to confirm this?'

'I have been by twice. Yesterday and again today. There was no reply to my ringing up to their flat.'

'You described a mansion flat. There must be a concierge or a porter?'

'Well, that is the odd thing. Yes, a porter, a funny little fellow. I tried, of course, but I could get nothing from the man, despite offering money. Even when I told him I had paid for the flat. That hardly impressed him.'

'You said you had given the flat to Reginald. That would make your son the owner.'

'Well, yes.'

'Then the porter's allegiance is to the owner. The new owner.'

'Outrageous.'

'No, loyal. It seems likely that Reginald must have gone somewhere, taking his valet with him, and rented or loaned his flat to friends. Some Londoners like to escape the holiday melee.'

'No. Reginald loves the damned holidays. Pardon my language. I cannot imagine it. I don't think he has any friends. Reginald devotes his time to artistic pursuits. He once told his mother he did not need friends. "With Michelangelo and Mozart, who needs friends?" or some such rubbish.'

Holmes raised an eyebrow. 'What of your two other sons? Did you buy them both flats in London as well?'

'That is none of your business. Attend to the matter at hand.'

'I am. Again, did you buy them flats in London also? Where are they at present?'

'No, I did not. I do not know exactly where they are. They—Robert is hunting in Scotland.'

'In December? *Brrrr.* And the other?'

'South of France. He has a . . . a lady friend.'

'They both keep in close contact with you? They let you and your wife know just where they are and what they are doing?'

The Marquis was silent for a moment.

'I see. Sir, what precisely is your worry? Reginald is of age. While his absence may be inconvenient, I fail to understand the extremity of your reaction.'

'It is just a feeling I have. I—this is so unlike him. Why would he let out his apartment and go off without saying anything?'

'The first is his right as the owner. And the second, his privilege as a man of independent means. Is there any jealousy, do you think, of the favoured son by his less favoured brothers?'

'No. Impossible. No, I cannot imagine. No!'

Holmes shifted in his chair.

'How concerned are you and your wife for Reginald's safety?'

'My lady is beside herself. I tell you, she is inconsolable. Crying round the clock. He would never desert her during the holiday. Not only is she worried, but she is missing all their little rituals. The mulled wine and biscuits. The garlands. The gifts. The spiced—'

'Stop!' Holmes waved his pipe in impatience. 'I suppose you would like me to find Reginald.'

'Do you taunt me, sir? It is obviously why I came. I want my son. I want him home safe. And in time for Christmas.'

'If he is in London,' I said, 'Mr Holmes will find him.'

Holmes shot me a glance of sharp reproof.

The Marquis seized upon my statement and leaped to his feet. 'Excellent, then! Confirm that he is safe, Mr Holmes. Let him know how much he has made us suffer. And make him write to his mother!'

'I am not a child-minding service, Lord Blandbury,' said Holmes with some asperity. 'However, as Watson seems to have committed me, I will locate him.' A pause. 'If he is not dead.'

'Dead? Good heavens!' The man went pale, and I wondered at this rather brutal comment from Holmes. The Marquis took out a handkerchief and made out to mop his forehead, surreptitiously dabbing at his eyes while doing so.

'My fee is two hundred pounds,' said Holmes.

I hid my reaction. Holmes rarely stated a fee in advance, and never one this high.

'Agreed,' said the Marquis. He walked over to the table by the door, took out a leather envelope from his jacket and wrote out a cheque, laying it on the table. 'Here is half, the rest when you find him. I am staying at the Langham. Report to me there.'

'Leave your son's address with Watson, Lord Blandbury. And in the meantime, do not approach his flat, and make no more attempts to contact him.'

'Well, I—'

'It is an absolute condition of my engagement on your case. And upon reflection, I must ask you to leave London today and return to your estate.'

'You ask too much. You cannot order me to—'

'That, too, is a condition.'

The Marquis reluctantly agreed and departed.

Holmes relit his pipe and sat thinking. I regretted my eagerness in volunteering his services.

At last, he arose and spoke. 'I believe this will be a simple matter. Although I would wager that the young man, wherever he is, does not wish to be found.'

'But what of this valet, Holmes? This George Perkins fellow? Might there be foul play involved?'

'We must satisfy ourselves to the contrary. But, Watson, I think it unlikely. Perkins promised to have Reginald write. If he were hiding such a thing, he would not have made that promise. I think it is far more reasonable to surmise that the two left for warmer climes and to be farther away from this overbearing father. Perhaps they loaned the flat to friends.'

'I suppose.'

'It will be a lucrative task for Heffie. Two hundred pounds can radically improve her life. I shall put her on the case.'

That was the explanation for the exorbitant fee. But he would discuss it no further. He dashed off a note and sent it via Billy the page to Heffie's latest address. Then he retreated into his bedroom, muttering in disgust, 'The mulled wine, the garlands, the gifts . . .'

At that moment, I thought I never knew a man so vexed by the holidays.

# CHAPTER 4

## *Madonna and Son*

he next morning dawned bitterly cold, and Baker Street glistened with a new snowfall, mounded along the sides of the road. Holmes spent the morning sunk deep in research among his many note-books and clippings and would not be engaged in conversation. I took another run at Pliny.

At a little after ten, Mrs Hudson and Billy, our page, approached the door to the sitting-room bearing between them an enormous basket of fruit with a red ribbon tied atop it.

'Mrs Hudson,' I exclaimed. 'Billy! Let me help you with that.'

I placed it on our dining table, where it took up nearly the entire surface. Against the background of Holmes's sombre quarters, it appeared like a sparkling pirate's treasure chest set out in a dusty library.

Oranges, pears, lemons, apples, grapes, currants, pome-granates and even peaches and plums were crammed in profusion into the wicker basket. On the top was a pine-apple. The out-of-season produce must have cost that same pirate's ransom.

'What a bounty!' I said.

Mrs Hudson smiled like a child on Christmas morning. 'Indeed, Doctor. And just in time. The larder, I am afraid, is a bit thin. Mr Holmes has been generous to his last client.' I briefly thought of Holmes's fee from the Marquis, but I knew I would not dissuade him from giving it to Heffie.

Handing both Mrs Hudson and the boy some fruit, I sent them off and removed the envelope to see who had sent this gift. It was a name I did not recognize.

'From the Endicotts, I presume?' Holmes emerged from his bedroom, dressing-gown over his other garments, finishing his tie.

'Yes. Who are the Endicotts?'

'Lady Endicott is the lady whom we helped in the street yesterday, Watson.'

'Oh! But I did not get her name. How did you divine this?'

'It was on one of three packages that fell from her maid's hands. Quite an interesting woman.'

'You were there but an instant, Holmes! The name, well, I see . . . but, all right then, how do you deduce that she is interesting?'

'I observe, Watson. One of the packages contained books,

unwrapped—therefore for herself. Philosophy, Darwin and Dickens.'

I shook my head in admiration. In the time it took to pull the child away from the attacker, Holmes had managed to note all this as well.

He gestured to Debrett's, lying open on our dining table. 'Of course, I have researched. Her husband is the second son of a Duke. Though she is apparently wealthy herself.'

'Kidnapping for a ransom, do you suppose?' I said.

'I do not theorize in advance of the facts, you know that, Watson. However, I wonder at this scoundrel's desperation.'

He moved to the window, pulled back the lace curtain and peered down into the street. Outside the snow drifted down in lazy flakes. 'If the lady is willing, I am inclined to insert ourselves into the matter,' said he.

'Offer our protection?'

'More than that. Find the man and see him gaoled. Giving her my card was an excellent move, Watson.'

'Well, the fruit is rather nice. But one cannot presume she knows or has looked up your profession.'

'She has.'

'How can you be sure?'

He stood at the window looking down at the street and turned to me with a smile. 'Because she is in the street below, looking for our address. So, thank you, Watson. I suppose my reputation has helped, just a little.' He darted into his room, pulling off his dressing-gown, and emerged a moment later in a neat frock coat, smoothing his hair.

Lady Endicott, along with her son Jonathan, soon stood

before us. Unencumbered by her winter coat and hat, and free from the terror of a recent attack, the lady's serene beauty was evident. She was of medium height, well-fed though not plump, and her golden hair was smoothed fashionably back from her face into an elegant braided chignon, with small curls in front. Her expensive dress of marine blue silk and matching hat conveyed the understated elegance of extreme wealth that does not need to announce itself loudly. The little boy, too, was carefully attired, but oblivious to the fact, as are all children.

'These are the two gentlemen who helped us yesterday, Jonathan,' said the mother. The child ran over to me, his arms wide for a hug. I bent down to receive it.

'Thank you, sir,' said the boy.

'You made quite an impression, Watson,' said Holmes.

Mrs Endicott smiled but reminded her son gently, 'Jonathan, darling, a gentleman shakes hands.'

The child backed up with a smile and extended a tiny hand. I responded in kind, delighted by the little one's instant poise. This formality accomplished, he dropped my hand and ran straight past me to the chemistry table.

'*Ohhhh*,' he squealed. 'Mummy, look!' He snatched up a small glass test tube filled with a clear liquid, upsetting some papers onto the floor as he did so.

'No!' said Holmes sharply.

'Jonathan!' cried his mother.

I leapt up, instantly scooping up the child. Holmes removed the glass tube from his hand gingerly, setting it down well out of reach. 'Sulphuric acid,' he remarked.

He and I exchanged a look.

As I returned the boy to his mother, I noticed a prominent port-wine stain on the back of the child's neck. It was at least two inches in diameter and in an unusual shape.

'I am so sorry,' said the lady. 'Jonathan, you know better than to touch things which do not belong to you.' While her reprimand was gentle, the boy paid close attention.

'Sorry, Mummy.' He turned to Holmes. 'Sorry, sir.'

She took Jonathan and placed him next to her on the settee. She caressed the back of his neck and looked up at me pointedly. She had clearly noticed me observing this mark.

'Yes, Dr Watson,' said she. 'I see you have noticed the "star". Jonathan has been blessed by this special gift—in the shape of a star. We think of it as the Star of Bethlehem. Jonathan was born on Christmas Day.'

'Well, then, a birthday coming,' said I.

'Yes, he will be four years old. A grand party is planned!'

As if on cue, the little one shouted in a high-pitched voice, 'Merry Christmas! Happy Birthday!'

Holmes, whose hearing was very acute, grimaced slightly, putting a hand over one ear. 'Lady Endicott, let us get to the crux of why you are here. I take it you know who I am?'

'I do. And I am now aware of just how lucky I was yesterday. Several of our servants have read of you, Mr Holmes, and my ladies' maid advised me to consult you.'

'Your maid?'

'Yes, Jenny reads those . . . those crime papers. *The*

*Illustrated Police Gazette* and others like that,' said Lady Endicott. 'They all do.'

'I see.'

'I would like to hire you, sir, discreetly, of course, to keep this man from us. And to bring him to justice. Or whatever it is that you do. Send him to gaol, I hope?'

'My *raison d'être* is indeed justice, Lady Endicott,' said Holmes. 'The police and the courts see the deserving to prison. Now, to the point. Do you have any clues as to the identity of this man? Did you recognize him?'

'No, I did not. But, of course, his face was mostly covered.'

'Did he say anything to you?'

'No.'

'He did not seem familiar in any way?'

'Not exactly.'

'What does that mean?'

The lady froze. 'I . . . I think I know what he wants.'

Holmes nodded. 'Obviously . . .' He gestured to the child who was engrossed in a clementine I had handed him. 'But why? Was this his first attempt?'

She looked uncomfortably at the little boy and paused. Finally, she enfolded Jonathan to her and covered his ears with her hands.

'I am not sure. That is why I am here. We had a break-in at our home.'

'When?'

'Last week. In the middle of the night. A masked intruder broke a kitchen window and made his way upstairs, but he was blocked by our butler.'

The little boy squirmed, giggling, trying to remove her hands.

'Did you see him?'

'No. But my husband thinks it has to do with some business dealings in France. And nothing to do specifically with our son.'

'Extortion, perhaps?' I exclaimed.

'Yes, yes, Watson. In light of your husband's concerns, madam, why did you not have the bodyguard with you yesterday? The young man who is currently hovering downstairs by our front door?'

'Mummy!' complained the child. She removed her hands from his ears. I moved to the window and looked outside. A young, solidly built, red-headed man of military bearing stood just outside our front door, scanning the street.

'Foolish of me, I suppose. My husband was furious. But I never dreamed that in public . . . in full view of . . .'

'The man who attacked you was clearly desperate,' said Holmes.

She looked up at us again. 'I have learned my lesson. Thank heavens you and Dr Watson were there to protect us. Hector, whom you see below, is well known in the family, a fine young man. He will not leave our side now.'

'I love Hector,' shouted Jonathan.

Holmes was silent for a moment, then stood and opened the door to the landing. 'Mrs Hudson!' he called out. He closed the door behind him for a moment and conferred with the landlady, then returned to the room. He bent down to the child and held a finger to his lips. 'Can you keep a secret, Jonathan?' he asked.

Jonathan mimicked the gesture. A game! The little boy then covered his own ears and, following Holmes, then covered his eyes, then his mouth, looking at his mother to do the same. She winked at him and covered her own mouth, then her ears. Jonathan squealed in delight.

'Jonathan,' whispered Holmes. 'Can you smell cinnamon? Our landlady has been baking, I perceive. A secret cake! Would you like some?'

'Oh, yes please!' said the child.

He looked up at Lady Endicott, and she nodded her approval.

'Watson?'

I rose and extended my hand to the child. 'Let's see about this cake,' I said. The boy nodded eagerly and took my hand.

'Have Hector join you,' said Holmes, as I led the child from the room.

I escorted Jonathan downstairs and directed Mrs Hudson to invite in the bodyguard. Behind her I noted a spiced cake cooling on a table. The smell was enticing.

Mrs Hudson smiled at me. 'There's some for you and Mr Holmes later, Doctor.' She invited Hector and Jonathan to sit, but before they could tuck in, Holmes's sharp voice rang out, calling me back upstairs.

In the sitting-room, Lady Endicott was standing, gathering her umbrella and coat.

'At three, then, Mr Holmes,' said she.

'Lady Endicott requests we visit her at home,' said Holmes. 'Lord Endicott seems to know more of this matter than he will share with his wife, and she is hoping we may entice it from him.'

'Certainly, madam,' said I. 'If anyone can get to the bottom of this, it is Mr Holmes.'

I accompanied her out, summoned a cab, and helped the lady and little boy inside. Hector followed, carrying two generous pieces of cake wrapped in waxed paper. He saluted me with one of them.

As they drove off, I wondered why the lady's husband would fail to warn his wife of apparent danger.

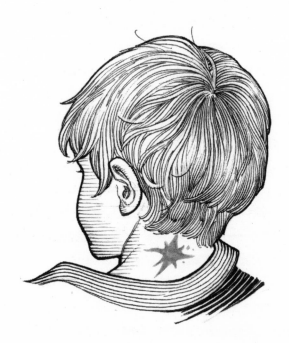

# PART TWO

## ANGELS SING

*'The only certainty is that
nothing is certain.'*
—Pliny the Elder

# CHAPTER 5

## *The Endicotts of Mayfair*

s arranged, we departed for the Mayfair home of Lord and Lady Endicott at a little before three in the afternoon. In the interim, Holmes had learned more of the Endicotts. His reliable notebooks, along with Debrett's, had informed him that our visitor's full name was Lady Andromeda Endicott, and that she was heiress to a vast fortune in dairy farms in Buckinghamshire, educated at Newnham College, and married to Lord Philip Endicott, who, in addition to being the second son of a duke, was a baronet in his own right.

While not set to inherit, Lord Endicott had made his own fortune through wise investments. He had numerous foreign interests and was active on the Continent, particularly in France, where he had recently been involved in some acrimonious and costly dispute over vineyard rights.

This could well be connected to the attempted abduction of his child. But before we could discuss this possibility, our cab pulled up to a large, handsome residence.

Two liveried footmen were positioned just outside the front entrance, and the butler, a blond man of my height and perhaps forty-five, athletic of build and supremely elegant, awaited us just inside. 'Mr Holmes and Dr Watson. Welcome, sirs,' he said, with a warmth visible beneath his professional reserve. 'My name is Jones. On behalf of us all here, we wish to thank you for your role in coming to the aid of Lady Endicott and Jonathan yesterday. Come, please. I shall take you to her sitting-room.' After a small bow, he led us to her.

Lady Endicott's sitting-room was exuberantly feminine, in pastel colours of peach and blue, with ornate, velvet-cushioned furniture from the last century. Jonathan sat on the rug nearby, busily constructing a complex castle from a collection of polished wooden blocks. The beautiful child was lost in concentration, oblivious to the adults around him.

Hector, the bodyguard, stood sentinel. I managed a closer look at the young man. His reddish hair was groomed straight back from his forehead in the stylish look favoured by so many young gentlemen, including, at times, my friend. His face had so many freckles that they blended into solid brown marks on his cheeks. He stood formally at stiff attention.

The lady arose as we entered and greeted us. Here, safe in her own setting, she shone like a jewel, a beautiful and patrician lady with a natural elegance. With a nod to Jones, she said, 'Gentlemen, I cannot thank you enough for your brave actions on Jonathan's and my behalf yesterday. You truly saved us both from the abyss.'

It was suddenly clear that her visit to us on Baker Street earlier in the day had been kept from most of the household. I presumed she had sworn Hector to secrecy. The butler departed and the lady smiled and nodded at Hector.

'It was a shocking attack, Lady Endicott,' I said. 'We are so relieved to see that you have both recovered.'

'This man here,' said Holmes, with a nod to Hector, 'and the two patrolling the front of your house, Lady Endicott— are they recent additions?'

'The new footmen, yes. My husband insisted. Gentleman, you have already met Hector Jones, who is now a personal bodyguard for my son. Hector will be at Jonathan's side every moment. He has been with the family since he was ten.'

Holmes smiled in sudden understanding. 'Except for his brief military service,' said he. 'Afghanistan, then, from the dates and the sun damage. Ah, I see that I am correct. Did you run away, underage, to the service, then return, realizing what you had here, with your father in his favoured position?'

The young man gaped in amazement at Holmes. The name 'Jones', of course, connected him to the butler. As for the rest, it was typical of Holmes.

'Indeed,' said Lady Endicott. 'Two years in Afghanistan. And yes, he ran away. We were fortunate to have him back. His father, our butler for many years, was greatly relieved.'

The young man by the door nodded to us deferentially and resumed his formal stance. A Queen's Guardsman came to mind. He needed only the tall bearskin hat to complete the picture.

'You said Lord Endicott demanded this protection, as the child's father?'

I found the wording of Holmes's question odd. His probe hit a target. The lady hesitated and shifted uncomfortably in her chair. 'Yes, as I said, he did.'

'It is natural to wish to protect one's son,' said Holmes, the emphasis on the word 'son'. The lady nodded, but I sensed discomfort. I wondered where Holmes was going with this.

'I have read, madam, of Lord Endicott's business dispute in France,' he said.

There was an awkward silence. Once again, the little one's presence was not suited for frank discussion.

'Perhaps, the boy . . . ?' said Holmes with a nod to Jonathan. 'If we are to speak openly?'

She nodded, then rang for a servant. A sweet-faced young maid appeared at the door and curtsied with a smile. Like every other member of the staff we had met at this house, she too bore a noticeably kind regard for her mistress.

'Jenny, please take Jonathan to the nursery,' said Lady Endicott, and the young woman happily gathered up the boy.

Jonathan shot a longing glance at his mother as he was led from the room. At the door he looked up at the young man. 'Are you coming, too, Hector?' asked Jonathan.

Hector nodded and chucked the boy under the chin. The child smiled in delight. Hector tapped a finger to his forehead in a kind of salute and followed them from the room.

Lady Endicott seemed to deflate. She took a sip of tea.

I noticed the snow continued to fall gently outside and my eyes wandered to the child's toys left on the floor, next to an embroidery frame by the window. Draped across the mantel, a twist of pine boughs, holly and ribbons in the pale peach and blue colours of the room added a discreet touch of the season. If it weren't for the near tragedy yesterday, this room would be a haven of wealthy domesticity. But unease pervaded the atmosphere.

'Lady Endicott,' said Holmes, 'The danger is not past. Considering the boldness with which this man attempted the abduction in such a public place—he is highly motivated. It is likely he will try again.'

She nodded numbly.

'I would like to know why your husband did not report the break-in here to the police.'

At this moment, a tall and elegantly tailored gentleman entered the room. His black hair, threaded with silver, curled attractively around a handsome, aristocratic face, which was long of nose, severe of mouth, and yet held a hint of humour.

'Philip!' exclaimed Lady Endicott, rising to greet her husband. As they briefly embraced, Holmes and I exchanged a look. This public display of affection was unusual among people of their class. But, I reasoned, the family was under duress.

51

The two turned to face us. 'And who might these . . . gentlemen be?' Lord Endicott asked, his eyes raking over both of us in an amused assessment of our status.

'These are the two kind gentlemen who came to my rescue yesterday. I invited them here, Philip. This is the esteemed detective, Mr Sherlock Holmes, and his friend, Dr John Watson.'

Lord Endicott expressed his surprise with only the slightest lift of his eyebrow. The lady had clearly not consulted her husband on the matter of calling in Sherlock Holmes.

'Mr Holmes, I have heard the name. Andromeda, you have invited them here for what purpose?'

'Why to thank them, of course,' said his wife.

'I thought we sent fruit.'

'Darling, I have since learned of Mr Holmes's reputation, I wished to consult him on the issue of last week's break-in.'

Her husband displayed no emotion. Turning to Holmes, he said, 'I am of course grateful for your and Dr Watson's kind actions yesterday, in comforting my dear Andromeda after the attack. And I believe you summoned a cab for her and my son?'

'Philip, darling, it was Mr Holmes who rescued our Jonathan from the man's clutches.'

'And pursued him through the crowds,' I added.

'Though failing, I understand, to capture the man,' said Lord Endicott. 'Pity. You have your reward and our thanks, but your services are not needed here.'

'Philip!' cried his wife.

'Someone broke into your house, last week,' said Holmes. 'Your wife is quite sure it is the same man. I can, perhaps, be of help.'

Her husband smiled. 'Mr Holmes, in deference to your favour to us, for I owe you no explanation whatever, I will tell you one thing. The intruder was clearly foreign—French, in fact. I have business dealings internationally, and I'm sure that incident was financially motivated.'

'It would be wise to pursue all avenues, Lord Endicott,' said Holmes. 'It is possible that these events are connected. Have you received any threatening communication from anyone?'

The man hesitated.

The lady nodded. 'Last week, Philip—'

'Andromeda! That is not your concern, Mr Holmes.' Lord Endicott turned to his wife. 'Darling, you should have consulted me before calling in this amateur,' said he. 'Pardon me, Mr Holmes, but that is what the newspapers call you. I have already in hand a renowned expert. Someone who will find and dispatch the despicable man who attacked my beloved and Jonathan yesterday. *This* man will not allow this criminal to slip through his fingers.'

'Sir—' I said, ready to come to Holmes's defence.

But Endicott held up a hand to stop me. 'He is here, and I wish to introduce him to you. All of France has sung his praises.'

Oh, no. *It could not be.* Holmes and I exchanged another look.

A tall, handsome, dark-haired man of about thirty-five

swaggered into the room. He was exquisitely dressed in the European style, looking for all the world like a diplomat from across the Channel. A small, well-trimmed moustache, brilliantined hair, and a permanent look of insolence completed the picture. He was a man Holmes and I knew well.

*Jean Vidocq.*

# CHAPTER 6

## *La Bûche de Noël*

y heart sank. The man had tangled with us more than once. He simply would not fade into the background. Persistent, like a bad rash. Vidocq, who advertised himself as a private detective, had falsely assumed the surname of the renowned (and long-dead) French policeman who had founded the Sûreté. The public, of course, assumed this fellow to be a descendant of the famous man, but he was not. Vidocq saw himself as Holmes's rival. He had managed to take credit for solving a wide range of cases on the Continent through a combination of trickery, lies and, in Holmes's estimation, a rather routine set of skills. Vidocq was a master of self-promotion.

And he had once knocked me down a flight of stairs. I felt my fists ball up at the sight of him.

Vidocq smiled. '*Bonjour, Holmes. Docteur. Quelle surprise.*' Insolence oozed from every pore.

'So thank you, Mr Holmes, Dr Watson,' continued Lord Endicott. 'As you now surmise, the situation is well in hand.'

'But Philip—' began Lady Endicott.

Holmes was not so easily dismissed. 'Has the man who attacked you in the street, Lady Endicott, or indeed anyone, attempted to abduct your child before this?'

'Well, I think it is possible that last week's break-in here and the incident on Oxford Street—'

'Andromeda, please,' said her husband.

But she would not be stifled. 'I think the two events are very likely connected,' persisted the lady. Newnham College in Cambridge was known for turning out very confident alumnae.

'I will attend to all of this, madame,' said Jean Vidocq. 'You forget that I was here at that time. I saw this intruder, and it was I who frightened him away.'

'*S'il vous plaît, monsieur,*' Lady Endicott said, ice in her tone. 'It was our butler and his son who frightened him away.' Out of the corner of my eye, I noted that her husband smiled in enjoyment at his wife's riposte. She turned to address Holmes. 'The man broke in through the kitchen window. But the strange thing was—'

'A common thief, after the silver,' intoned Vidocq. 'But he was not successful.'

'No,' said Endicott.

'Why do you assume he was a thief?' asked Holmes.

Vidocq smiled unctuously. 'Me? Why, like you, Mr Holmes, I *assume* nothing, but infer from detail. But in my case, with wisdom and experience.' He tapped his forehead. 'The odds tell us so. One does not look to the zebra when the horse supplies the explanation.'

'Nothing missing in the butler's pantry? The silver, for example?' asked Holmes.

'No,' said the lady. 'Nothing was taken.'

'It is kind of you to concern yourself,' said Endicott. 'While I appreciate it, we have the matter well in hand. If perhaps you—'

'Odd, if he came in through the kitchen and thievery was his motive,' mused Holmes. 'What was it that you deemed "strange", Lady Endicott?'

'He had made his way upstairs,' said she.

'I see. What time was this?'

'Two in the morning,' said the lady.

'To your bedrooms? Where you would be at that time. Your rooms are upstairs, on the first floor?' asked Holmes.

She nodded. 'They are. But—'

'*Naturellement*,' said Vidocq. 'Having found the silver locked away, one might surmise that he transferred his target to the lady's jewellery, which would, of course, be found in her private rooms. That is an exquisite coral and diamond necklace, by the way, my lady.'

She put her hand to her neck self-consciously.

'Why attempt this burglary while they were at home? Why not while they were out—at the opera, for example?' said Holmes.

'I leave the house infrequently,' said the lady. 'You met me at a rare moment.'

'*Why* do you not leave the house, madam?' asked Holmes.

'I . . . I so enjoy my son. I do not like to leave him in the care of servants. I know it is an unpopular view, but I believe children benefit from a strong maternal presence. And so, when I do go out, Jonathan goes with me.'

'Not precisely relevant,' said Vidocq, with a dismissive Gallic shrug. At the lady's sharp look, he bowed slightly. 'If you will forgive me, madame.'

'Please continue with your description of the break-in,' said Holmes. 'Did the intruder seem interested in your jewellery, Lady Endicott?'

'No, not that either. Because he continued up the stairs—'

'And is the nursery on the floor above your rooms?'

'The second floor, yes.'

'Holmes, you pursue nonsense,' said Vidocq. 'Lord Endicott has engaged me to take care of an unpleasantness which has arisen from his businesses in France. This has nothing to do with you. It is well in hand.'

Lord Endicott seemed relieved to drop the subject. 'We are grateful for your action in Oxford Street, Mr Holmes, and you, Doctor. But I ask you both now to leave us. Good day.' He looked towards the doorway. 'Jones.'

The butler was there, present before being summoned in the prescient way of the well-trained servant. I thought I caught a look of dismay but it was instantly replaced with practised neutrality. Jones gestured politely in the direction of the way out.

Holmes moved to the door and I followed. But at the

threshold, he turned back. 'Is your son adopted by chance, Lord Endicott?'

'Good day, Mr Holmes,' said Endicott, icily. Behind him Jean Vidocq smirked in triumph.

'This way, sir,' said the butler.

As we approached the front of the house, Holmes hung back and addressed the fellow. 'Jones, if you do not mind, I would like to have a look at the point of entry where the intruder breached the house, if I may?'

Jones nodded silently and brought us to the kitchen. Once there, with the door closed carefully behind us and a footman set outside it to watch for the family, he turned to my friend. 'Mr Holmes, you will understand my need for discretion. But we below stairs are all in favour of your being brought in on the case. We have read of your remarkable achievements and frankly are concerned for the safety of the family, particularly young Jonathan.'

'You agree with me, then, that abduction *was* the goal of the break-in?'

'You did not hear it from me, but yes, I thought as much even before Lady Endicott's misfortune yesterday. The man stole nothing but went straight away to the second floor where the nursery is.'

Holmes nodded as he bent to examine the bottom of the window where the intruder had gained entry. Even I could see that it had been patched up with a new lock and several slats of wood, but evidence of the violent break was still visible, made with a crowbar or similar.

Holmes stood. 'The man brought tools with him. Careful

planning. See the marks here and here. But now this is well-fortified, I would look for other vulnerable points of entry.'

'It has all been done, quite thoroughly, sir. New locks. Added fortification, and a night watchman.'

Holmes stood up from examining the window lock. 'Excellent. You confronted him just outside the nursery. If he is the same man who attacked Lady Endicott yesterday, he is a younger man, with a good thirty pounds and six inches on you. Was that the case?'

'Yes.'

'Masked, of course?'

'Yes.'

'Did you by chance notice a small scar over the right eyebrow?'

'Indeed I did, sir!'

'What happened then?'

The butler hesitated.

'Were you armed?' asked Holmes. 'As you are now?'

The man started.

'I can see the outline of what I presume is a Derringer in your waistcoat pocket, there.'

The butler nodded. 'Yes, sir.' He revealed a gun secreted in his elegant jacket. 'I had it with me in the pocket of my dressing-gown. I pulled the gun on him, but he attacked my son Hector and escaped down the back stairs.'

'And are you usually flitting about the house, armed, in the middle of the night?'

'Only recently, sir. A maid heard a noise and alerted me.'

'Then you have not always been so armed?'

The man hesitated. 'No. Only since Tuesday last. It was after Lord Endicott received the second of two letters.'

'Interesting. The dates of these letters?'

'The seventh, and then another on the eighth. The handwriting was the same on both.'

'Excellent. And the content of these letters?'

'I am not in the habit of reading his lordship's correspondence.'

'No, of course not. But—'

'I can only say that they greatly upset his lordship.'

'Was there a return address?'

'No, only a post office. Two different post offices, both in Aldgate.'

'Where are the letters now?'

'He burned them, sir.'

Holmes frowned. 'When did this fellow Vidocq arrive?'

'On the ninth. Oh, and he had a look at the letters before Lord Endicott burned them. I caught the end of their discussion. 'The man creates a fiction,' said Monsieur Vidocq. 'It us undoubtedly connected to "*L'affaire Renoudet*". That is, of course, the matter upon which he was summoned.'

Holmes looked thoughtful.

'I hate to be disrespectful, but our French guest fills me with unease,' said Jones. 'There is something—'

'Indeed. Good work, Jones. And the date of the break-in?'

'The next evening. The tenth.'

'I am curious about one point. What evidence was there that the intruder was French?'

'Monsieur Vidocq, as I said, was in residence here at the

61

time. He awoke and was standing on the landing below when my son and I confronted the intruder on the second floor. Monsieur Vidocq said the man exclaimed "*Sacré Bleu*" as he ran from us down the back stairway.'

'Did you hear this as well?'

'I did not hear "*Sacré Bleu*"—except from our guest, Monsieur Vidocq. The intruder himself said, "Bloody hell!"'

Holmes smiled. 'Our old friend Vidocq. He plays true to form, concocting nonsense to impress upon his client the need for his services. I doubt this break-in had anything to do with "*L'affaire Renoudet*", whatever that may be. What happened next? How did the man escape?'

'My son and I raced after the fellow down the back stairs, but he was very fast. A footman intercepted him in the basement and attempted to remove the mask, but he too was struck down. The villain ran into the kitchen.'

'Slippery devil!' I exclaimed.

'He surprised the kitchen maid who was doing the morning baking and then overturned a pot of boiling water to block pursuit. It barely missed her, but the footman slipped and fell. The fiend seized the moment to dash away.'

Holmes frowned. 'What did the police make of this attempted kidnapping? Despite our friend Vidocq's theory, it seems the obvious reason for the break-in.'

'The master did not call in the police.'

'Odd. And no trouble before this?'

'None. I believe Monsieur Vidocq was invited to investigate a potential litigation with this man named Renoudet. Nothing more.'

'Thank you, Jones. I shall follow up on this. Just one more question. Lord Endicott did not see fit to warn his wife of whatever danger he sensed?'

The butler looked downcast. 'He did so, but very lightly. She did not take it seriously. I believe he did not wish to alarm her.'

'She strikes me as an eminently reasonable person and not prone to overreaction. She felt safe enough to venture out yesterday with only her ladies' maid. That implies she knew little of the threat.'

Jones did not wish to make a personal comment but his slow nod told us all we needed to know.

The snow was heavy, and a footman summoned a cab while we waited under a portico. Jones walked us to it, holding a large umbrella over our heads.

'I sincerely hope you will continue this case, Mr Holmes,' said he.

Holmes nearly smiled. 'That is my intention. I agree that kidnapping is the likely motive. I will take it upon myself to track down this man and see him brought to justice. Oh, but one more question. Is Jonathan adopted, by any chance?'

'I am unaware of such a thing,' said Jones, stiffly.

Holmes regarded him closely for a few seconds. 'Fine. Take every care. This man will try again, more boldly. Be on your guard.'

# CHAPTER 7

## *Heffie's First Report*

t was nearly five when we returned to 221B, and already dark. Heffie awaited us, and as we entered the room we found her seated by the fire, a book in her hand, eating an apple, no doubt from the enormous fruit basket on the table near her. Holmes smiled at this.

I was surprised at her presence so soon. Holmes had set her on the case of the Marquis of Blandbury's missing son only yesterday.

She looked up at us with a smile. 'I 'elped myself to an apple, hope that is agreeable to you, Mr 'olmes.'

Holmes smiled. 'Heffie, I gather you have news for us. What have you discovered about the elusive Reginald Weathering?'

She put the apple and the book aside. 'Sorry to report,

but there ain't no sign of 'im, Mr 'olmes. Only that feller George Perkins is still there. 'E's been in and out, with a lot of nice Christmas food and things coming in, and pretty dresses.'

'Dresses! So, it would seem to be the valet Perkins and a paramour,' said Holmes, settling into the armchair opposite Heffie. 'Have you seen her?'

'Yes. Not too clear, though.'

'You're sure the man there is George Perkins, the valet?'

'Unless there's two Georges. I followed 'im to the butcher's and 'eard him give 'is name. But he ain't dressed like no valet. 'E's dressed like money. Bespoke. Very fine stuff indeed.'

'Good work, Heffie. What about Christmas decorations? Pine boughs, gifts?'

'Yes, all of that. Wreaths. A tree, even,' said she. 'A little one.'

I wondered at this question, which struck me as irrelevant. I plucked a clementine from the basket and began to peel it.

'Describe the lady, please,' continued Holmes.

'I've only seen her up in the window, through some lace curtains, not any kind o' detail, sorry. And she ain't never gone out, least not while I was awake.'

'What can you tell me of her?'

'Not much. Can I have some grapes, please?' she added, eyeing the fruit basket.

'Take what you want,' Holmes said, waving at it dismissively.

Heffie got up and examined the enormous basket with interest. 'What is this thing?' she asked.

'It is a pineapple,' I said. 'Surely you've seen a pineapple?'

'Only pictures. And this?'

'I believe that is a papaya.'

'Any good?'

I shrugged. I had only read of papaya.

'Take them,' said Holmes impatiently. 'And let us return to a more fruitful discussion.'

I groaned, and my friend pressed on.

'The lady. What have you seen of her, precisely?'

'Not much. She's never so much as opened them lace curtains. I've only seen her silhouette. She's a slender one. Tiny waist. Lot o' hair, worn up.'

'All right.' Holmes frowned. 'Did you visit?'

'Tried to.'

'What did this lady have to say?' I asked.

'She won't answer the door when this George feller ain't there. I tried. Then I tried when 'e were there, like I had a message for the wrong address, of course. 'E opened the door a crack, but 'e wouldn't let me see behind 'im, blocked the door.'

'I wonder that she won't answer the door,' I said. 'How does she accept mail and deliveries?'

'There's a porter 'oo takes in all that,' said Heffie.

'Did you speak to the porter?' asked Holmes.

''Course I tried. What do you take me for? Porter won't talk. So I went upstairs and knocked on Reginald's door a third time after I saw this George feller leave, 'opin' to speak to the lady direct. She would not let me in.'

'Then you *did* speak to her?'

'Through the door. Only a couple of words. She seemed sad.'

'What do you mean, sad?'

'Like she been crying.'

Holmes and I exchanged a glance. This did not bode well, I thought. I wondered if this mysterious woman was somehow being held in the flat, showered with gifts from the inexplicably wealthy servant. A bird in a gilded cage, as the saying goes.

'Anything else, Heffie? Did she have an accent?' asked Holmes.

'Upper-class accent. Something were up, I could tell. Maybe I looked scary through the little 'ole in the door. Though I was wearing one of them nice dresses, too.'

'Perhaps it was *your* accent,' I suggested.

'No, I did my veddy heducated voice,' said Heffie, in her very educated voice.

Holmes laughed, but then said, 'Heffie, we need more. I'd like you to continue your surveillance. I need you to have a close look at the lady, get her name if you can.'

The girl looked chagrined, but only for an instant. 'Righto. I'll try again tomorrow. I got an idea.'

She stood and tied up the fruit into her winter scarf, creating an impromptu knapsack. She was nothing if not resourceful.

I rose to get her coat and held it up for her to put on.

'Heffie, if you can do your very educated voice, why do you say "one of them dresses"?' This came out before I could think better of it.

Heffie looked at me as though I had just suggested she disrobe. 'Because I am who I am and proud of it,' said she. 'It's like a costly dress. It's not me, but I can wear it.'

She shrugged on her coat indignantly.

'Well, you are many things, Heffie,' said Holmes. 'Do not be afraid to embrace your intelligence. To disdain educated speech is a kind of reverse pretence. But I understand. Meanwhile, be very careful what you do next. There could be danger. We do not know what is at stake here. Do not break into that flat.'

''Ow'd you know that were my plan?'

'Because I know you, Heffie.'

'Something ain't right there.'

'I suspect that your instincts are correct. Consider that there may have been a crime, that this lady may have been crying because she is held against her will. And we do not yet know what happened to the gentleman in question, Reginald Weathering. Discretion, Heffie. Observe but do not interfere. Promise me.'

'All right, Mr 'olmes,' said she, disappointed. 'If you insist.' She left the room.

At the window, Holmes and I watched her make her way down Baker Street. A gentleman, after doffing his hat to a lady, then moved out of the way in avoidance of Heffie.

Holmes sighed and shook his head.

'She is an impressive young woman,' I said. 'I do regret,

however, that a young lady of her intelligence does not attend to her language. So many more doors would open to her.'

'Watson, you know better. She said it herself. She does not feel "like herself". Although I have hope for Heffie. I have never met a more able autodidact.'

Beneath us a four-wheeler disgorged two gentlemen wearing fashionable but perhaps overly loud clothing. One reached into his pocket and removed a large wad of bills, peeling one off for the driver, who looked surprised at the amount. He tipped his hat deferentially in thanks.

'Perhaps we should take a page from the Americans,' continued Holmes. 'Like those two. They would have no trouble admiring Heffie and would most assuredly treat her as a lady. Class is less visible to many of them.'

'Unless they are wealthy young ladies seeking to marry for a title,' said I, thinking of the strange fate of Lady Pellingham, née Miss Annabelle Strothers, in a case I had written up as *Art in the Blood* sometime earlier.

'Yes, yes, Watson. But cynicism does not become you.' He shook his head. 'We English are all locked into precon- ceived notions of our station in life, based on nothing more than an accident of birth.'

'Well, it is an age-old system, although you seem to be little hampered by it,' I said. Holmes, by his clothing and speech, was clearly a gentleman.

'Not so, Watson. You have repeatedly seen me having to establish my credibility. And my profession? *Ha!* It is a joke to some.'

'Until they have need of your help.'

The carriage below departed. The two young men consulted a paper and looked up and down the street.

'I hope they are not coming here,' I said, thinking that two cases were enough at this time of year.

'They are not. They are visiting young Dr Renfrew, who has hung his shingle just over there.' He pointed in the direction of a chemist's down the street.

'Yes, above the chemist's, as you said. But how do you know they are visiting the doctor?'

'Renfrew is a specialist in skin rash. The second gentleman, the one in the rather insistent green tartan coat, is nearly writhing with discomfort and trying not to scratch his neck where a red irritation shows above the starched collar. See?'

Of course, he was right. I immediately felt an itch at the thought.

'Those rashes, once they start, they spread everywhere,' he remarked.

I said nothing. Perhaps I squirmed slightly.

'The time of year. Dry overheated air. Scratchy wool. Around the neck, particularly,' said Holmes. He eyed me curiously. 'Or bedbugs.'

I could bear it no longer and gave my neck a good scratch.

Holmes laughed. 'Watson, sometimes you are too easy.'

# CHAPTER 8

## A Constellation

he next day passed uneventfully and on the morning after, I awoke to that peculiar blue light that heralds a deep snowfall during the night. I remained for a moment in the comfortable bed in my old room in Baker Street, as the familiar scent of Mrs Hudson's fine coffee drifted up from our sitting-room. As I dressed for the day, I eagerly looked forward to my friend's thoughts on the two cases on our horizon.

Even though the Endicott imbroglio was not precisely given to him as a case, he had taken it on without a doubt. It was not the first time he had assumed a case without a paying client. The vulnerable child and his lovely mother had clearly ignited his sympathy, and something about Lord Endicott's reluctance to discuss the incidents had set off his curiosity.

But Holmes was not to be found this morning. Instead, beside the pot of coffee on the dining table, lay two things. One was a sealed note on what I recognized as his brother Mycroft's stationery, and next to it one of Holmes's notebooks, open at an article he had pasted in there quite recently. It was dated the fourth of December this year.

I poured myself a coffee, picked it up and read.

'Marylebone Workhouse Scandal! Babies stolen and sold!' screamed the headline. 'Following a spectacular trial which took place over the last several weeks, Mrs Claudine Huron, late of the Marylebone Workhouse Children's Services, has been sentenced to ten years' hard labour for masterminding a diabolical scheme. Infants born in the workhouse were wrested away from their true parents and apparently sold to the highest bidder.'

I went on to read how this 'fiendish woman told vulnerable couples, already devastated by being separated in the workhouse, that their newborn infants had died. But in fact these infants were placed in elite adoption agencies.' Two agencies were named: The Children's Haven and Bright Little Ones. The article went on to say that the court concluded that fees were paid for these adoptions and Mrs Huron's personal circumstances were under investigation.

Could it be that Holmes suspected that Jonathan was one of those stolen infants and that the kidnapper might well be someone involved, or at the very least interested in taking advantage of this situation? And might this situation have triggered both the break-in at the Endicotts' and the

Oxford Street imbroglio? It seemed unlikely. It would mean a destitute father from the workhouse was behind these aggressive and frankly daring attacks. And if he was set upon this path by the article, as I supposed the dates might suggest, he would be literate. Few workhouse denizens fit that description.

I poured myself another cup of coffee and sat down to read today's papers.

Sometime later, I heard the door open below, and in a moment my friend bounded into the room, his pale cheeks reddened by the icy weather.

'Watson, remind me never to refuse well-paying work, lest we both end up in the workhouse! I know they are a necessary evil, but my God, what a dreary and sad place. And practically on our doorstep.'

He had just returned from the Marylebone Workhouse, the largest in London, and one which was less than a four-minute walk from our door.

*His* door, I reminded myself.

'Life saving, however,' I pointed out, thinking of the many of London's destitute who would starve or freeze in the winter without such shelter. 'And you are forgetting, I do have my medical practice, Holmes.'

'Oh, well, of course. But perhaps you should turn to treating rashes. Renfrew is making a killing. Take note of that consulting room above the chemist. Referrals!' Holmes grinned at me as he knelt before the fire, rubbing his hands in the warmth.

'I read this article that you left, Holmes. What did you

discover at the workhouse? Is it your theory that Jonathan may be one of the stolen infants referred to here?'

'Good, Watson! Your time with me has not been wasted.'

'But a rather distant theory, is it not, Holmes?'

'Look at the date of this article.'

'I have done so. *Ah* . . . I see. Wasn't that a few days before Lord Endicott received the letters?'

Holmes grinned. 'Excellent Watson! Soon you will be tracing new constellations in the heavens. Well, of course it was. And while you call it a "distant theory", if Jonathan Endicott was indeed one of these stolen infants, then the facts do offer a credible explanation for the chain of events. Hence my visit to the workhouse.' He shrugged. 'The trial and this lurid article precisely fit the timeline.'

'That is quite a leap.'

'Perhaps. But follow along. Mrs Huron, the lady mentioned in the article, is a woman of legend there. In his desire to shock, this journalist has painted only a part of the story. What I learned at the workhouse was this: during her long tenure as head of children's services there, Claudine Huron was something of an evangelist in improving care for the infants and small children trapped in the workhouse system.'

'Not the villain as described in this article, then?'

'No. Mrs Huron was instrumental in improving children's educational offerings at the place, instituting sanitary practices into the birth process and care of newborns—in short, a tireless champion for the welfare of the most vulnerable workhouse residents. People who worked with her there are utterly aghast at her sentencing.'

'And yet she kept these children apart from their parents?'

'That was not her doing, and also not entirely true. There were communal accommodations for newborns and their mothers there. Created by Mrs Huron, I might add.'

'How, then, was she accused and convicted of such an egregious transgression as selling the children of living parents? And did she actually commit such a crime?'

'It was not proven that money changed hands. At least not as far as Mrs Huron is concerned. The solicitor Rudyard Click was successful in returning one child to the mother who gave him birth.'

He sat down at the breakfast table and poured himself a cup of coffee, taking a large swig. 'Ugh! Cold!' He set the cup down with a rattle.

'And still . . . an improbable connection with the Endicotts, Holmes,' said I, unconvinced that the Huron case and the Oxford Street incident were related.

'Improbable, but not impossible. I intend to pursue it.'

'How?'

'Imagine, for a moment, that you are the father of an infant who was born in the workhouse. But you are told that he had died. By some miracle, or perhaps diligence, you manage to get work. You and your wife escape the workhouse and begin to remake your lives . . . and then you read this.'

'That presumes a lot. For example, that the kidnapper can read. Rather long odds, are they not?'

'Yes, Watson. The father must be literate, of course. It narrows the odds somewhat, but not immeasurably.

Consider that he happened to read this article. And that the birth and purported death of his child must *exactly* fit the timeline of what we have seen.'

'Yes . . .'

'What would you do, Watson, if you were such a parent?'

'Well, I might be inclined to . . . to investigate.'

'How might this train of thinking lead to the Endicotts? It may well be this mysterious father who is the intruder in the night. But how? How did he know where to go?'

'Why, it *is* a mystery!'

'Think, Watson, think. What would you have done?'

'Well, I, er . . . I suppose I would wish to read the court records. Perhaps some details would reveal themselves.'

'Precisely. In addition to the workhouse, I have been to the records office this morning. I have read the entire transcript of the trial. No names of workhouse parents were included in the transcripts. Nor the names of any of the adoptive parents. Of course, getting those transcripts took a bit of doing—it is unlikely that our mythical villain could have done so. But look here. Two adoption agencies were named in the article.'

'Well, then, I would go there, of course,' I said.

Holmes lifted the lid on the tureen that had contained scrambled eggs. I had polished them all off. He set it down with a clatter.

'But Holmes, how likely are these agencies to give up the names of the adoptive parents to anyone?'

'Not at all inclined would be my thought. But no matter. That is where we will start.'

'Might we not simply ask the Endicotts?'

'Did you not remark that I already did? They will not admit it. Adoptions by some are considered a stigma, a failure on the part of the wife to bear children. The butler was unwilling to weigh in on this issue, but you saw his hesitation, did you not? Even if they did admit that the boy was adopted, I would wager they do not know his true story . . . if he was, indeed, one of the children snatched and sold.'

I nodded. Given the timing of the letters—just after the trial had hit the papers—it might well be connected. Vidocq's zebra, perhaps. Holmes's idea held credence.

'Consider, Watson, if this theory is correct, the abductor is desperate, furious, and—judging from the glimpse I got of his eyes—possibly emboldened by drugs or alcohol. Certainly determined and perhaps even looking for revenge. In any case, he is a danger. He risked what may be his own son by grabbing him in a crowd, intending to run through the ice—'

'But if the man *is* Jonathan's real father—'

'Then I suppose one can argue that he is in some way deserving of at least a legal appeal. This in no way excuses his violence. But we get ahead of ourselves. We must find this man and get to the truth before he harms someone in his desperation. Or succeeds in abducting the child.'

'We have so little to go on.'

'We shall follow the leads we have. We are left with two places to begin, and those are the two adoption agencies named in the article. Dress warmly, Watson. We leave in ten minutes.' His eyes alighted on the envelope near the butter dish. '*Ah*, a note from my brother.'

He opened it, read it quickly and chuckled.

'Something relevant to the case, Holmes?'

'More or less. The French problem of Lord Endicott— "*L'affaire Renoudet*"—was due only to a misunderstanding at a bank. The "scandal" was just some journalist's conceit. It will be put to bed by this evening.'

'When did Mycroft have time to discover all this?'

'Yesterday. It was the work of only an hour or two.'

'Then Vidocq is completely superfluous!'

'As is often the case. And lends weight to my theory that the letters had nothing to do with the French situation, despite what Vidocq said to Lord Endicott.'

Mrs Hudson, with her almost prescient and kind attentions to my friend's needs, appeared in the doorway with a fresh pot of coffee and a tray of scones.

'Fresh coffee, Mr Holmes. But I will not leave it without a promise that you will eat a morsel.'

He frowned up at her like a naughty child, but she, like a firm schoolmistress, set her jaw and would not enter the room with her bounty.

'All right, Mrs Hudson. You are a tyrant.'

'Only when required,' said she.

# PART THREE

## GLORY TO . . .

*'With man, most of his misfortunes*
*are occasioned by man.'*
—Pliny the Elder

# CHAPTER 9

## *Nutcracker*

or such an unsociable man, Holmes seemed to be effortless in attracting allies as needed. Just as the butler Jones was inclined earlier to his side, before the day was over we obtained help from a coffee proprietor, a baker's apprentice, a secretary and a prisoner. Despite this notable ability, however, Holmes had few actual friends. I have often considered that I am perhaps his only true friend.

We began by setting out to visit the two adoption agencies mentioned in the news article. It would be a remarkable piece of luck if the would-be abductor turned out to be the father of Jonathan, and even luckier if he had identified himself to the agency in an effort to track his stolen child. It seemed unlikely to me, but Holmes deemed it worth a try.

The first agency, The Children's Haven, was located not far from us in Marylebone, easily within walking distance. As we proceeded east on Paddington towards the fabled medical enclaves of Harley and Wimpole Streets, Holmes abruptly stopped in front of a small coffee house.

'A hot chocolate, Watson, I am a bit chilly,' he said, rather loudly, and opened the door of the shop.

This was unlike Holmes, but he darted inside, and I followed. Once there, he waved at the proprietor in a familiar manner, and the man waved back. He very rapidly propelled me to the back of the shop and we slipped out of a back door into a small mews.

'Holmes, why—?'

'We are being followed, Watson.'

'I saw nothing!'

'Of course not. Come with me.'

In a trice we had exited the mews, turned right, and doubled back to Paddington, emerging several doors east of the coffee house. Holmes pulled me into a doorway and cautiously peered towards the place we had just left.

Hovering across the street from the coffee house was a familiar figure in a well-tailored overcoat and a dashing black Homburg. The tall man was fixated on the entrance to the coffee house. It was Jean Vidocq.

Holmes shook his head ruefully. 'As I thought, the lazy fellow! He hopes to solve the case by our efforts yet again. Wait here, Watson.'

'You are not going to try to reason with him, Holmes? The man is a danger, or he can be.' Not only had he knocked me down a flight of stairs, but I later witnessed his formidable fighting prowess in a street brawl in Paris.

'Reason with Jean Vidocq? You know me better!' From his coat he withdrew a small notebook with a silver pencil attached. He smiled as he scribbled a note and handed it to me. 'Head back the way we came. Find a child or a beggar and pay him this to deliver my note to our French friend.'

'A child or a beggar? Where will I find this willing messenger?'

'Be creative.' He added three pieces of silver to the note. 'This will make someone's Christmas a happy one. Then, as soon as Vidocq has left, proceed to The Children's Haven. Wait for me there, Watson. Do not enter.'

With that, he vanished back into the empty mews.

My curiosity got the better of me, and I opened the note.

*V.—I am on a different and far more lucrative case, and will leave you to the Endicotts. But I have information you can use. Meet me at the south end of Paddington Gardens, and I will share what I have found.—SH.'*

Within moments I discovered a young apprentice of perhaps twelve, scraping ice from the windows of a bakery. I convinced the lad to take two minutes from his work to do my bidding. His face lit up upon seeing the silver. 'Yes, sir!' he said.

Five minutes later I reached the address of the first adoption agency. I was dismayed to read on a notice pinned to the door that it had closed permanently. Holmes was nowhere to be seen. I waited five, then ten minutes, stamping my feet to keep warm. The sky grew dark with clouds and I knew it would soon snow again. Through the windows of a restaurant across the street I observed diners who seemed to be enjoying hot soup. Breakfast, though recent, seemed long past. I considered going over there to wait when at last my friend appeared.

'Holmes!' I exclaimed at the sight of him.

His very fine beaver top hat (that I had long coveted) was smudged with grime on one side. A red welt showed above one eye.

'Fisticuffs, Holmes? Will that man never cease to cause trouble?'

Holmes smiled. 'Consider him duly challenged. I believe he will have a difficult time explaining the state of his own face to his new employers.'

I laughed. Holmes rarely engaged in physical tussles, but when he did it was usually no contest. Years of semi-professional boxing and proficiency in baritsu were just two of his attributes. An uncommon strength for such a thin man was another.

'But surely Vidocq will be retained until Mycroft reveals the facts?'

'My brother will have already informed Philip Endicott this morning. The sooner London sees the back of Jean Vidocq, the better.'

'By Jove, you Holmes brothers have been swift!' I declared.

But Holmes's delight was short-lived as he then read the note regarding the closure of The Children's Haven. If they had information that would help in the Endicott case, we would never find it now.

'Onward, Watson, to Bright Little Ones. Let us simply hope that the Endicott adoption, if indeed Jonathan was adopted, took place there.'

Bright Little Ones was located on a side street in Belgravia, adjacent to a French hairdresser, who must have catered only to the elite, judging by the elegant gold-lettered sign and the beautifully attired lady we saw entering. A discreet but well-polished brass nameplate revealed the agency's existence.

A stairway led to the first-floor offices, and alongside it on richly panelled walls were several oil paintings, impressive in their gilded frames, all portraying rosy-cheeked, happy children or, in one case, a mother and child. It seemed to be a kind of advertisement for the wares.

Prominently at the landing hung a large painting of a rather self-satisfied boy in a blue silk suit of the last century, staring out at the viewer in utter confidence.

'Gainsborough's Blue Boy,' said Holmes. 'A decent enough reproduction.'

Entering the office, we were greeted by a prim male clerk with a flamboyant orange cravat. Holmes gave our names. The young fellow looked up in surprise.

'Mr Sherlock Holmes? *The detective?*' the young man whispered, awestruck. 'Only your surname is on our appointment list for today! Surely you do not wish to adopt a child? Or do you? I have read of you, sir! You have my deepest respect. James Halbrook at your service.'

At this stage in Holmes's career, public recognition was rapidly increasing, but not always a given. 'Thank you,' said he. 'How long have you been employed here, Mr Halbrook?'

'Nine months, sir. Three months before Mrs Turner took over.'

I could sense Holmes's disappointment at this. But there was a hint of discontent in the young man's voice, and Holmes seized upon it. 'Perhaps you can help me, then? I read that the manageress four years ago was a Mrs Pettigrew. I had hoped to speak to her.'

'Passed away. A wonderful woman. Ran the business since 1873. Mrs Turner was her assistant for years. Apparently, she . . . inherited the place.' That last had a tinge of bitterness.

'This does not seem to please you, Mr Halbrook.'

The young man looked uncomfortable but nodded. He glanced nervously in the direction of the inner office.

Holmes lowered his voice to a whisper. 'I *am* here on a case, as you have so cleverly inferred. Can you keep a secret?' Smiling, he put a finger to his lips.

The clerk, delighted to be invited into a conspiracy, mirrored the gesture, and said, *sotto voce*, 'Happy to be of service, sir.'

'How does the agency support itself? I presume the adoptive families are wealthy. The fees to adopt are sizeable, I presume?'

'Indeed, sir. Of course, that is also to ensure the adopters could generously provide for a child. Mrs Pettigrew was highly selective.'

'Where do these children come from?'

'I am not privy to that on an individual basis. But I believe from a variety of sources, both city and country. Parents who are dead, impoverished, or unable to care for their wee ones. It is all in the files.'

'There must be papers to be signed, then, if the birth parents were alive?'

'I suppose.'

'And the new owner—Mrs Turner—is she equally selective about those who wish to adopt?'

The young man's face tightened. 'Things are different,' he said. 'Criteria have changed . . . and prices, er, fees have gone up.'

'I do not follow.'

'Well . . . some children now are placed more for, er, a variety of reasons.'

'*Hmm.* Well, I hope to locate files on a particular adoption of four years ago. I believe it was a Bright Little Ones affair.' He leaned in and spoke softly. 'A dangerous criminal has surfaced with claims on the adopted infant. This child is now in peril.'

James Halbrook's eyebrows shot up in alarm. 'Dear me!'

I wondered at the wisdom of this gambit from Holmes. I should not have, of course.

'Though you were not employed here at that time, do you know if there are records still extant?'

'Oh, yes. But Mrs Turner would never allow—'

'Mrs Turner would never allow *what*, James?' came a woman's voice behind us.

We turned to see a tall, pale woman in her late thirties standing in the doorway. She was elegant in a slim-fitting, grey dress with a ruffle at the neck. She had an Italianate face—long-nosed, with prominent cheekbones, flashing black eyes and the curved lips of a Roman statue. Quite a stunning woman, I thought, not conventionally pretty, but with a remarkable sense of style.

'Ma'am,' said James, 'I was just telling Mr Holmes here that you would never allow an adoption without thorough investigation of the adopting couple.'

'Well, of course not.' She stepped forward with a warm smile and extended her hand. 'Mrs Olivia Turner,' said she. 'Mr Holmes, I believe? And you are?' She turned to me.

'This is Mr Watson,' said Holmes.

I smiled but wondered at the 'Mr'.

'Follow me, gentlemen.'

We were ushered into a luxurious office, where a fire burned merrily in the hearth and two velvet chairs faced a large, polished campaign desk. Mrs Turner took her place behind it. A tall window to one side of the desk looked out at the graceful brick and white-trimmed façade across the street. Snow drifted down picturesquely, clean and white. Even nature seemed kinder in the more expensive areas of London.

Mrs Turner eyed us carefully. 'How can I help you, gentlemen?' Her black, wavy hair was elaborately coiffed into a chignon with a profusion of curls down the right side of her face. Perhaps she was a client of the French hairdresser next door. I was glad that Mary did not go in for such extreme fashion, although Mrs Turner wore it well.

Holmes looked thoughtful, then glanced at me. He turned to the woman. 'We are looking to adopt a young girl,' said he. 'But I believed we were to speak to a Mrs Pettigrew.'

Mrs Turner kept a small smile fixed upon her lips, as though she intended to convey a kind of benign helpfulness. 'Mrs Pettigrew has sadly passed on,' said she. 'She contracted influenza from—from somewhere—and departed this earth last July. But I can help you.'

'I see,' said Holmes, disappointed. 'Let us be hopeful. I will need you to assure us that any child we might adopt is free and clear of any encumbrances. Or illnesses.'

Yet again we were somewhere under false pretences, and Holmes had not seen fit to warn me. There were times when I thought he was simply improvising. But he had made an appointment. I wondered what my role was to be here.

'Encumbrances?' questioned Mrs Turner. 'Whatever can you mean, sir? All our children are carefully checked for illness and temperament. That is why we have the reputation that we do. Only the best for the best.'

I had once bought a bull pup from a dog breeder with a similar rhetoric.

'You can assure me that there will be no parents to emerge from the woodwork and lay claim to the child we receive?' asked Holmes.

'Out of the question. As I said, we research our children

thoroughly.' Without a blink, she added, 'And the adoptive parents as well. We are a reputable agency, Mr Holmes.'

'But the influenza?'

Mrs Turner sniffed. 'That sad occurrence happened when Mrs Pettigrew was out visiting a prospective adoptee in unusual circumstances. It was there she contracted—but never mind. Any child you receive from us will have been carefully inspected.'

'Inspected?' said Holmes. '*Ha!* I am reassured, then.'

'Your wife, sir? Usually both prospective parents interview with us.'

'I will have to do,' said Holmes crisply.

Mrs Turner took this in her stride. 'Certainly, sir. Tell me more about what you are looking for. Age? Sex? Do you have a particular temperament in mind? Playful, inquisitive, respectful, docile?'

'Oh, docile, of course. "Shy" would be excellent. A female only, aged ten to twelve. And sturdy. We will provide for her, of course, but she will have duties,' said Holmes.

Mrs Turner returned the smile. 'Understood. I am sure we can find you a suitable girl.'

'However, if you are careful, don't you want to know a little more about me?' said my friend.

'I observe, Mr Holmes. I can see from your clothing that you are a sombre, serious man, and from your immaculate grooming that you are respectable, neat, responsible and orderly.'

I fear that I made a small noise at 'orderly', and both turned to me. I cleared my throat.

Mrs Turner resumed, 'The quality of your garments tells me that you can afford the care and upkeep of a child. You listed your profession as a banker on your application yesterday.'

Yesterday! Holmes *had* been busy.

She smiled, proud of herself for these keen deductions. She then turned to me. 'And who might you be, sir?'

'Mr Watson here is my solicitor,' said Holmes.

At last. I attempted to put on my most solicitor-like mien.

'But still, Mrs Turner?' said Holmes. 'You haven't even asked if I am married.'

'But of course you are, sir. Your exquisite grooming, your fingernails, the lack of even a spot of dust on your frock coat. A woman notices these things, you see.' Mrs Turner beamed at us both. 'Someone is looking after you. And now you know our secret. I am a kind of detective!' She smiled flirtatiously.

Holmes beamed back at the woman. 'So I see,' said he.

'And there is more,' continued Mrs Turner. 'You certainly have the means to support one of our special, bright little ones, Mr Holmes. Only a substantial citizen could afford a private solicitor to join him on such a visit.'

'You are perceptive, madam,' said Holmes. 'But as I am a careful man, perhaps you can first set my mind to rest about this.'

And it was at this point that the meeting took a sharp turn into uncharted waters.

# CHAPTER 10

## Less Than Bright

olmes removed from his breast pocket a folded-up newspaper clipping and opened it, laying it upon the desk in front of Mrs Turner. It was the article about Mrs Huron and the scandal of the Marylebone Workhouse, and the 'orphans' who were not actually orphaned.

The woman glanced down at it and turned pale. She pushed the paper back towards Holmes. 'That has nothing to do with Bright Little Ones,' said she. 'That woman! Simply awful! No! All our children are orphans. This is carefully checked. The reporter is mistaken!'

'Really? It names this agency in the article as one of the sources of the stolen children,' said Holmes. He folded up the paper and put it in his breast pocket.

'Do you believe everything you read in the newspapers?' said Mrs Turner.

'I suppose not,' said Holmes amiably. 'Thank you for assuaging my doubts.'

'Let us turn to your needs. I can offer you Felicia, a charming girl, twelve years old, who shows promise in the culinary arts, if that would please?'

'Interesting! How much would you charge me to adopt Felicia?'

Mrs Turner smiled. 'Our fee for placing this girl with you is one thousand guineas. We will offer you a discount if you pay in cash.'

Holmes's eyebrows shot up. 'My! And you are entirely certain she is unencumbered?'

'No family in the world. Felicia is one of our more valuable orphans,' said Mrs Turner. 'We have paid to have her apprenticed with a cook. That is why our price, er, *fee* for adoption is so high. I have turned down several offers for her.'

'Well, then, a bargain,' exclaimed Holmes. 'What do you say, Mr Watson?'

By now, of course, I had realized Holmes's approach. The meeting had certainly taken a strange turn.

'A bargain indeed,' I said. 'The girl can cook, you say? Because, as you can see, Mr Holmes is sorely in need of better nourishment.'

Mrs Turner smiled as she regarded my excessively lean friend. 'You will eat like a king!' she exclaimed.

Holmes seemed to hesitate, considering.

Mrs Turner lowered her voice and leaned towards him. 'And the girl will be very amenable, to whatever sir desires.'

Holmes inhaled sharply, then smiled. 'Why yes, Mrs Turner, I believe I understand you completely. But before we come to an agreement on Felicia, are you familiar with a little boy, adopted out as a newborn four years ago, and originally rescued from the Marylebone Workhouse? A rather unique little boy. Born on Christmas Day. A port-wine stain in the shape of a star on the back of his neck?'

Mrs Turner stiffened. 'We do not take on infants with obvious flaws. They are hard to place. Why do you ask?'

*Obvious flaws.* My opinion of Mrs Turner could not be lower.

'The adoptive parents were Lord and Lady Endicott, and I see from your reaction that you remember them,' said Holmes pleasantly. 'They told me themselves that they adopted their child from Bright Little Ones. That is why I am here.'

Of course, they had done nothing of the kind. He was bluffing.

'While we are glad for the referral, Mr Holmes, we do not discuss prior adoptions.' Mrs Turner tried a different smile. 'Our clients rely on our discretion. As can you, as well.'

James Halbrook had quietly entered the room and began filing papers in a tall wooden cabinet on the wall behind Mrs Turner.

'Mr Holmes, are you inclined to take Felicia, or not? I

can have her here to meet you later in the day. But I have another couple who have already expressed interest. You must act quickly if you want her.'

Holmes smiled. 'Mrs Turner, before we discuss Felicia further, I must continue on the subject of this little boy. He was most certainly adopted from this agency and is now in danger from a violent man, who somehow has tracked him to the Endicotts. Has anyone else made an enquiry about this child in particular?'

'I don't recall.'

'I believe he may be representing himself as the father of the child in question. He has attacked Lady Endicott in the street.'

The boldness of Holmes's fishing expedition should not have surprised me. If his theory were correct . . .

'Surely you exaggerate, sir?'

'No. I witnessed the attack. A tall man, about my height, but heavier and younger. A small scar above the eyebrow, here. Pale blue eyes.' Holmes observed the woman closely. 'He has not been by to see you—on some premise or other?'

Mrs Turner tapped a silver pen repeatedly on her pristine desk. 'As I said, I don't recall.' Even I could sense her lie.

'Well, in any case, he would hardly have given you his real name. The Endicotts wish to find him and bring charges against him. They feel endangered, and justifiably so.'

'Try elsewhere,' said Mrs Turner, giving the pen one more sharp tap. She set it down. 'Now, about Felicia—'

'The Endicotts have not forgotten where they adopted

their child,' said Holmes reasonably. But a vein in his forehead pulsed and I sensed the fury beneath the calm. 'And
that the child came from the Marylebone Workhouse.'

'We don't take in such children. If you are so sure, why
not inquire there?'

'I have. Won't you check your file for me, please? As a
favour to my friend, Lord Endicott?'

'It will not be there. We purge our files every two years.'

Behind her, the young clerk continued with his filing. He
looked over at us with a frown and shook his head in
contradiction, almost imperceptibly.

'Madam, I must insist.'

'How would this help you? What if this meretricious
claim were true? Would you wrench the boy from his
adopted family and throw him into the gutter, then, with
his birth parents? Including—if you are not mistaken about
this—a ruffian who attacked someone on the street?'

Holmes drew back, his face cold and hard. 'Your concern
is touching, particularly in light of your attempt to sell a
young girl to me as something more than a cook.'

Mrs Turner stood, her face white with fury. 'You have
come here under false pretences, Mr Holmes. I shall report
you to the police!'

'Be my guest, madam. Let us indeed bring in the law.
Mr Watson here will verify that you have proposed not an
adoption, but to sell a twelve-year-old girl to do my personal
bidding. The inference will be clear in any court of law.
You may as well try to sell the girl to a bordello.'

'No!'

'You will get no less than ten years if I report this. Perhaps more.'

Mrs Turner's smile had turned into a rictus. 'Get out!'

On the pavement in front of Bright Little Ones, we stood hoping for a cab. Few were in view. The wind picked up and a wet snow came down in flurries. At last, a four-wheeler appeared at the end of the street, and Holmes blew his whistle to summon it.

'That went well, don't you think?' I murmured, viewing our visit as a total failure.

'Abominable woman. Sadly, it will take more than our evidence to convict her. But, by God, I'll see this place shut down,' said he.

The four-wheeler pulled up. I moved towards it, but Holmes stopped me with a hand on my arm. I followed his look to see a beautiful lady emerge from the coiffeur, her hair protected by a silk scarf, with a young man holding an umbrella to shield her. Holmes gallantly invited the couple to take our cab. The lady smiled her thanks, and a pungent waft of perfumed oils drifted our way as they passed us.

'That was kind of you,' I remarked, shivering as the four-wheeler pulled away. 'Holmes, what now? She will destroy the file before anyone can get a warrant. And my misrepresenting a solicitor will not help your case.'

'Patience. I need a moment longer,' said he. 'Try for a cab, would you, Watson?'

Aggrieved, I stepped into the street to do so, but a sudden hiss behind me drew my attention. James Halbrook had emerged from the Bright Little Ones doorway and remained under the portico, beckoning to Holmes. He joined him and they exchanged some words. I could see Holmes's disappointed reaction. Nevertheless, he reached into his pocket and handed the young man some silver. James Halbrook bowed his head in thanks.

Once again, Holmes had created an ally in the instant.

A few moments later, I had secured a less desirable hansom, and we began our freezing ride northward. Next to me, Holmes sat silent, his face dark with frustration. At last, he spoke.

'We have all but confirmed it, Watson. It seems our villain has been here before us. He is a resourceful man. Our friend James Halbrook said a man fitting the description came by four days ago but was rebuffed by Mrs Turner. That night the office was broken into, though strangely nothing of value appeared to be taken. The agency keeps its files arranged chronologically, and those of four years ago were discovered scattered across the carpet. Mr Halbrook, of course, refiled them . . . and while we were there, he attempted to locate the Endicott file.'

'Behind that harridan's back!' I exclaimed.

Holmes smiled bitterly. 'Yes. It was missing.'

'My God, Holmes, your theory seems to be correct. '

'You have a gift for stating the obvious, Watson. Lady Endicott's attacker has been here before us. This is how he found his target.' Holmes struck the side of the cab in frustration. 'I must have the fellow's name—and find him before he tries again!'

The cab turned towards Baker Street and Holmes suddenly rapped on the ceiling with his umbrella. 'Cabbie. Rye Prison, if you would,' he shouted up at the man.

'Right-o, sir,' came the reply, and we made a right turn at the next corner.

'Watson, it is time to speak to the one person who may identify the father to us.'

As we turned north towards this ominous place, the wet snow continued to seep its way into our cab, even through the protective hood of the hansom, as it always did at this time of year. I shivered, perhaps less from the bitter cold than from the anticipation of the place where we were now headed. It was where the worst female convicts were held, the sister prison to Pentonville. And one of the saddest places in London.

# CHAPTER 11

## *The Matron*

y the time our hansom arrived at the north end of Islington, Holmes and I were both shivering, the wet snow having penetrated every small gap in our winter clothing. We alighted at the entrance to the women's prison. Enormous iron gates separated the community from this dismal edifice. If the inside was anything like Pentonville, then the convicts ranging from petty thieves to the murderous were incarcerated in dank and freezing cells, many under forced labour sentences, toiling under great duress.

I assumed it would be difficult to gain entry to speak to any of the inmates. Yet, without delay, we were admitted to confer with the prisoner, Mrs Claudine Huron. Apparently, the director of the prison was another in Holmes's network of allies.

We passed through a courtyard where thirty female prisoners were taking their brief exercise, silently walking in a circle as the snow whitened their drab prison garments. No trace of holiday cheer had leaked into these bleak surroundings.

If the inmates had been sentenced to hard labour, some may have been forced to spend hours on the treadmill or sitting in desolate rows, not allowed to speak. Others were set to pick oakum, working till their hands bled. Perhaps worse, some were obliged to turn a large metal crank, alone in their cells, until they collapsed in exhaustion. I did not know which of these dire punishments were given to women.

Hard labour was like a slow death sentence, as many perished from the physical strain, or were driven to fatal despair by the sheer pointlessness of the tasks to which they were assigned.

Soon we found ourselves in a small, cold room with several chairs, a high, barred window and one door. Seated rigidly on one of the chairs, her right hand handcuffed to the wooden armrest, was a large, pale creature of perhaps fifty, her thin grey hair loosely tied back from her forehead, then secured in a sparse knot. Her careworn face was that of a once handsome woman, now transformed into a forlorn, bloated version of her former self.

This was the notorious Mrs Claudine Huron, formerly matron in charge of the nursery at the Marylebone Workhouse.

Her grey prison uniform fitted her badly, but despite this, and her present shameful circumstance, the woman sat erect in her chair, proud and unwavering. Her pale green eyes burned with the righteousness of a missionary.

We sat down before her and Holmes introduced us both, mentioning his profession.

'Mrs Huron,' said he, 'I am here to ask for your assistance.'

Her lips twisted into an angry shape that might have been a smile.

'Assistance? How can a prisoner in my state help you?'

'I am in the process of trying to protect a little boy. A child whom you, too, may once have tried to help.'

She barked a laugh. It came out more like a cough.

'You may not believe me, Mrs Huron, but I am sympathetic to you,' said Holmes. 'I am familiar with the details of your trial.'

'*Ha!* The newspapers were wrong!'

'No, I read the full transcripts of the court proceedings. I do believe you,' Holmes continued, 'when you said that you were quite literally saving lives.'

'They were all orphans. All of 'em,' she said belligerently. 'You'll never hear otherwise from me.'

'Mrs Huron, please. The solicitor, Mr Rudyard Click, proved beyond all doubt that in *at least two cases* you put up for adoption children who were born in the workhouse and whose mothers survived. The law did not take kindly to removing children from living parents without their knowledge or permission. You were playing God, as the courts saw it.'

'What do you want?'

'I have seen first-hand the conditions of the workhouse,' said Holmes. 'I have witnessed the desperation, addiction, despair, turpitude and even blatant criminal behaviour.'

Mrs Huron laughed, though without a trace of humour. 'You have not seen it as I have.'

'What do you mean?'

'The children in question were in danger of their very lives.'

'I believe you, madam.'

She snorted. 'You may well, in theory. Yet many more believe that the original parents deserve sovereignty in all cases. And thus . . . here I am.'

Holmes continued, undaunted. 'I have come to help a specific child. He is four years old. He was adopted as an infant less than a month old from an agency called Bright Little Ones, and the adoptive parents were told he came from the Marylebone Workhouse.'

'Adoption agencies frequently lie about their sources.'

'I have reason to believe this child came from you. And I hope this is true.'

'Why?'

'Because then you can tell me what I need to know. An extremely violent man has attempted to abduct this boy from his adoptive parents. My theory is that he believes himself to be the real father and rightful guardian. I must find this man.'

While we were not sure of the content of those letters, I well understood Holmes's need to press on with the theory.

She shrugged and stared resolutely at him.

'He failed, I presume?' she said. 'And what if he is the

real father? And this child was under my care—what if this is true? Might he not attempt to reopen this case through your interference?'

'Mrs Huron, even if he does, you cannot be tried twice for the same crime,' I offered.

'I speak not for myself. In any case, the law has seen fit to call me a criminal. I will die in this place. Meanwhile a violent man wants a child he claims is his. Where is the justice in all of this?'

'Mrs Huron, I agree,' said Holmes. 'But the issue of justice for the child, for the birth parents, and for the adoptive parents, is indeed a complex one. Surely you can provide evidence?'

'I have already tried. In many cases I was the only witness to the threats against these helpless babes. Very young children and their mothers were isolated at the workhouse and placed directly under my supervision. One sweet infant, only days old, nearly died when the mother left him on the cold floor of her cell as she slumbered in an opiate-induced stupor nearby. I was barely able to stop another mother from beating her toddler to death over a crust of bread. The court would not hear me in full.'

Holmes nodded. 'It is truly shameful that they did not. I may have some influence to re-open your case.'

The woman started and glared at Holmes. 'Do not dare to do so!'

'It can hardly go worse for you, madam,' said I.

'Oh, yes it can,' said the woman, and fear darkened her face for just a moment.

'She is right, Watson,' said Holmes. 'And yet, madam, I think not, if your full testimony could be heard.'

'Understand this, Mr Holmes. I would never have stolen an infant from a fit mother. But I have been pilloried in the newspapers as having acted out of sheer prejudice because the parents were "disadvantaged". Popular opinion falls on the side of the original parents and I've been accused of discrimination.'

'The truth is often nuanced,' said Holmes.

'Nuanced? Don't be a fool. Those children would have perished!'

Holmes and I sat silent.

'Go away. I am resigned to my fate. I will die here in this place, but in the highest court I will be redeemed.' Once again, that strange light shone from her eyes.

'Madam, please hear me out,' said Holmes. 'The child in question was adopted by a very wealthy couple here in London, Lord and Lady Endicott. The boy is much loved by them and happy in his new home. He is thriving. I believe he was one of your special cases.'

'If it be so, then *finis coronat opus*,' said the prisoner with a shrug. She smiled to herself.

My schoolboy Latin surfaced murkily in my brain. The phrase meant 'the end crowns the work', or better, 'justifies the means'.

'Ovid. Yes, Mrs Huron, but as I said, the truth is nuanced. However, in this case, perhaps not,' said Holmes with a quick glance to me. 'The adoptive mother, Lady Endicott , and her maid were knocked to the ground in broad daylight in Oxford Street two days ago in a violent attack. The man wrested this same adopted child from her arms and nearly escaped with him.'

'Surely not?'

'I was there. The attacker escaped in the crowd.'

'It was Mr Holmes who saved the child,' I pointed out.

'This action in Oxford Street is only the most recent in this man's attempts to steal the boy,' said Holmes.

Mrs Huron shifted in her chair. 'Children are regularly stolen and sold. Kidnapping is a more likely explanation. You cannot connect this villain to me.'

'Oh, but I can,' said Holmes. 'The timing indicates that it is precisely tied to you. The papers made a meal of your story, as you know. Two nights after this story broke, a man fitting the description of the Oxford Street attacker visited the Little Bright Ones adoption agency and asked after this adoption but was turned away. That night there was a break-in and their files were ransacked. This man thus found the Endicotts.'

Mrs Huron looked away, desperation in her eyes.

'Letters greatly upsetting to the Endicotts followed, presumably from this man.'

'Where posted?' asked Mrs Huron.

'Both letters had post offices as their return connection. That lead is now gone. In any case, Lord Endicott did not notify the police. Two nights after the last letter, the Endicotts suffered a break-in by a masked man of my height, but heavier. Pale blue eyes, a small scar over the right eyebrow. Thankfully he was repelled by the servants.'

The woman frowned as if trying to pull an image from memory.

'You know him, madam? He will stop at nothing, and it is only a matter of time. If my theory is correct, this man either is, or believes he is, the father of the child in question. I need a name.'

'You seem resourceful yourself. Why not find a way to entrap him?'

'Use the child as the lamb to draw the tiger, Mrs Huron? Never. I will seek the tiger in his lair.'

'To what end?'

'Obvious. To ensure the safety of the boy.'

'Then you, too, play God. What if the man *is* the father? Consider how the courts may view this desperate man. He feels justice is on his side. Have *you* never committed violence in the name of justice?'

Holmes was silent.

He had, I knew, committed violence to protect others. And at least twice that I knew of, he allowed violence to take place without stopping it. Baron Gruner and Charles Augustus Milverton came to mind. In each case I could not fault his logic, nor the correctness of his decision.

Mrs Huron regarded us closely. 'I recognize a fellow crusader, Mr Holmes. But it can all go so terribly wrong. The birth father—with the help of someone like that "do-gooder" solicitor Rudyard Click—may be able to sway public opinion with the argument of rightful paternity. Do not underestimate the willingness of the courts or the public to decide a child's fate without all the facts.' Her eyes burned into Holmes's own.

'But they must decide in favour of the Endicotts!' I exclaimed. 'Jonathan is so happy, so loved.'

Mrs Huron tore herself away from staring at Holmes and turned to me. Her face softened. 'Tell me more of this child, Jonathan,' said she. 'Four years old, you say?'

Holmes sat silent. He gestured to me to supply the description.

'His parents dote on him,' I offered. 'He is a sunny little boy, as all four-year-olds are, but something more. It is as though he brings light into every room he enters. His mother, unlike others of her class, includes him completely in family life. He is filled with laughter, with joy. A birthday celebration is being planned for him next week. He was born on Christmas Day. There is to be a party on the eve—'

'Christmas Day?' Mrs Huron sat forward in her chair, her eyes burning once more. 'Tell me, does this child have a port-wine stain on the back of his neck?'

'Why, yes,' I said. 'In the shape of a star.'

Mrs Huron gasped and raised her free hand to cover her mouth. We waited. I was about to speak, but Holmes held up a hand to stop me. The woman's composure had been breached at last. She breathed heavily, struggling to control her reaction, and her eyes glistened with tears.

'I know this child. Christopher is his name. His birth name,' she said. 'When you described the father, I was not sure, but . . . oh, dear God. It *is* Christopher.' A tear coursed down her cheek and she rubbed it away.

Holmes and I exchanged a glance.

She paused, finding the words difficult. 'Christopher was . . . he was a special one. Even as a newborn. Something about him. He had an almost angelic quality. The other children cried constantly. But when I put Christopher in the cot next to them, they quietened instantly. He . . .' She drifted off, awash in memories. The tears now flowed freely down her face. I handed her my handkerchief, which she took it gratefully. 'Sweet. So incredibly sweet. We only had him a matter of weeks.'

'Did you name him, Mrs Huron?' I asked.

'No, his mother did. He was born on Christmas Day. Therefore . . . Christopher.'

Holmes glanced at me. Confirmation at last.

'The mother's name?' asked Holmes.

Mrs Huron shook her head. 'Clarice. A child herself. Barely fifteen, I think. She was very possessive, but a danger to her infant. Addicted to opium. She defied regulations and secretly took him from the nursery to her own quarters. Christopher was the child left on the cold floor by his mother. He was nearly dead when he was found.'

'My God,' I said, picturing the happy, well-fed little one now.

'What of the father?' pursued Holmes.

'The father . . . They were kept separated, as the work-house does. Strange fellow. I remember him vaguely . . . he was a once a successful man. Formerly some kind of engineer, having to do with ships, I think. From up north. He could not tolerate being separated from his wife in the workhouse. He pined for her, insisted he saw the good in her, and hoped to cure her. As I recall, he kept getting work and then losing his position. His temper was legendary. Alcohol was his demon. And now that you mention it, yes, he had a scar on one eyebrow.'

'A name, Mrs Huron!' cried Holmes.

There followed a long silence. Somewhere in the cell, or perhaps within the wall, was a steady drip. The cold floor sent shafts of ice up our legs.

'Findlay,' she said at last. 'His name was Peter Findlay.'

'Thank you, Mrs Huron.' Holmes sprang to his feet and rapped on the barred door to summon the guard.

Mrs Huron slumped in her chair. For a moment I thought she had passed out—or worse.

'Mrs Huron?' I said, crouching down beside her and placing a hand on her shoulder.

She looked up at me, and her tear-stained eyes burned into mine. 'Please,' she said, 'tell me I did not make a mistake in giving you the name. Tell me that, above all, you will keep the boy safe.'

'That is precisely what I intend to do, Mrs Huron,' said Holmes. I heard the scrape of metal on metal as the door was unlocked by the guard.

I took one of her hands in mine. 'Sherlock Holmes is a man of his word,' I whispered. 'He will do right by this boy.'

Mrs Huron nodded and closed her eyes.

In the cab en route to Baker Street, I wondered how,

precisely, Holmes would manage to protect the boy, now knowing the truth. Would the law—would public opinion—support what was best for the child?

And what *was* best for Jonathan?

# CHAPTER 12

## *Heffie's Second Report*

e returned to 221B to find Heffie sprawled on the settee, reading, her boots off and resting by the fire to dry. She had certainly made herself at home. To my surprise, she was engrossed in Pliny while eating a banana from the basket.

She looked up with a grin as we entered.

'Do make yourself at home,' said I.

'Yes, do. Both of you,' said Holmes with a smile.

Of course, I, too, was but a visitor. It was easy for me to feel at home at the address where I'd lived for so long.

'Sorry,' said Heffie, reaching down to put on her boots.

'How are you finding Pliny?' asked Holmes, picking up the book from where she had set it down on the table. 'I see you've progressed further than Watson.'

'It says 'ere he had a "romantic death". What in 'eaven's name is that?'

'He died by inhaling a cloud of debris and poisonous gas from the eruption of Mount Vesuvius,' I said, knowing at least that of Pliny.

'Yes, but what's romantic about that? You could die of the stink in 'ere and it would hardly be romantic.'

The vestiges of Holmes's chemistry experiments still lingered.

'The story of Pompeii is a great tragedy,' explained Holmes. 'Pliny went there to study the event and increase scientific knowledge.'

'No. I still say he went on a rescue mission,' I said.

'*Oh*, you two. You each think this Pliny bloke was like you,' said Heffie.

I laughed at her unexpected bulls-eye.

'Tell me what you have found, Heffie. I presume you somehow spoke to the woman staying at Reginald Weathering's flat?' said Holmes.

Heffie's face fell. 'No, and there's been a development. This George Perkins feller, 'e's an odd one. Been busy, like buying up all o'London. Fortnum and Mason, loads of victuals, then dresses. And jewellery. The man's rich, I tell you. I thought you said 'e were a valet?'

Holmes picked up his pipe and lit it. 'That is correct, Heffie.'

'Well, I don't know any servant with that kind of money,' said she. 'Or maybe I'm in the wrong business meself.'

116

'All of these luxury purchases—did he buy anything for himself?' asked Holmes.

'Oh yes, indeed he did. Savile Row, no less! I'm not on 'im every minute, of course, but there must be more, because now when 'e's about town, 'e's much, much better dressed.' She shook her head. 'And I s'pose 'e's gettin' much better service in the shops. I followed 'im into one on Jermyn Street, and they were all over 'im like butter on toast.'

'Still no sign of Reginald?'

'No one's come in or out of their flat,' said she.

'And the lady has never emerged?'

'Not on my watch,' said Heffie. 'Seen 'er in the window, though.'

'It is peculiar,' I said. 'His wealthy employer vanishes. A sudden fortune.'

'But what is this *development*, Heffie?' asked Holmes.

Just then Mrs Hudson entered with a tray and three steaming mugs of hot mulled wine. Heffie and I took ours with delight, but Holmes waved her away. 'Not now, Mrs Hudson, we are working!'

'It is the Christmas season, Mr Holmes, and time for you to take a pause,' said Mrs Hudson.

'I am busy. Go away!'

'Holmes!' I took his cup and placed it on a table by the fire. 'Thank you, Mrs Hudson. And your spiced cake was delicious,' I added.

'Gingerbread next,' said she.

Holmes groaned in impatience and the landlady smiled

as she left the room. She was well used to Holmes and his ways.

Holmes turned again to Heffie. 'The development, Heffie?'

Heffie took a large slug of her mulled wine, and started to wipe her mouth with her sleeve, caught herself, and withdrew a delicate hankie and used that instead.

'As I said, the lady 'asn't shown 'er face. And this George feller, 'e's a petty thief. Quite good at it,' said the girl. 'Lifts little things from shops, even ones 'e's spending loads of cash in.'

'A petty thief, then. I do not like this,' said Holmes thoughtfully. 'What is your theory of the lady? Do you think she may be held prisoner?'

'Maybe. Maybe not.'

'Explain.'

'Well, it's just an impression I 'ave. I saw them embracing once. It looked . . . well, it looked *more* than friendly. I would say it looked like . . . love.' She paused. 'Not that I've ever—'

'Through the lace curtains? Then you only saw their silhouettes?' asked Holmes.

'Yes. I keeps 'oping they'll open those, but no luck.'

I shook my head. The situation was puzzling.

'The question remains, where is Reginald Weathering? He seems to have been replaced by the man's lady love,' I said. 'And all this spending?'

'Do you think foul play, Mr 'olmes?' asked Heffie.

'Some kind of play, to be sure. Heffie, you said "maybe" and "maybe not".'

'Yes. I can't say why I ain't sure, but somehow—'

'I'd like you to cease your surveillance, please. You have been most helpful.'

'Just like that?' asked Heffie with a frown. 'You want me to stop?'

'I do. And thank you.'

'What you going to do, Mr 'olmes?'

'Watson and I will pay a visit tonight.'

The girl looked disappointed.

'I have another assignment for you, Heffie,' said Holmes. 'Have you the time?'

'I do. It's a bit slow at Scotland Yard just now.'

Holmes took a slip of paper from his desk and scrawled something on it. 'I need to you to locate a man named Peter Findlay. He has worked, in the past, likely as a maritime engineer trainee, or something related. He teeters on the edge of utter poverty, has trouble with alcohol, but is educated. He is tall, about my height but heavier, has a scar over his right eyebrow, and pale blue eyes. I estimate twenty-four or twenty-five years old.'

''Ow urgent is this, Mr 'olmes?'

'Extremely, Heffie. And the man is dangerous. Find him but stay well away. I mean that. He can be violent. He is likely to be married and living somewhere in the vicinity of, or perhaps between, the two post offices I have written there. I need his home address.'

She nodded. And with the addition of several more tropical fruits to her stash, she seemed happy. And yet . . .

Heffie paused at the door. 'Mr Holmes. About this George and his lady. And the missing Reginald feller?'

'I will take it from here,' said Holmes.

Heffie sighed. 'I would like to—'

'No.'

I saw her lingering glance as she departed. I did not trust her entirely to keep clear. I took another swig of Mrs Hudson's concoction and felt its warmth spread through me. No, she would not heed Holmes. Of that, I was sure.

# PART FOUR

## THE NEWBORN KING

*'From the end
spring new beginnings.'*
—Pliny the Elder

# CHAPTER 13

## *Bird in a Gilded Cage*

utting Heffie on the trail of Peter Findlay had been an inspired choice. Her contacts in the East End and her ability to move freely and pry information from its denizens made her valuable to Scotland Yard, and in this instance to Holmes. She would, Holmes informed me, locate this man far faster than he would. And this, he reasoned, would give us time to pursue the Marquis's missing son.

The next evening, he said, we would confront the valet, George Perkins, in his lair.

'I can't imagine he will let us in,' I said.

'We must ensure by whatever means that he does, Watson. I have more concern than I expressed to Heffie. The sudden wealth. And yet thievery raises issues. The hostage possibility. The situation is odd.'

Holmes then asked me to prepare for our visit by dressing in my finest clothing. As I had to return to my house to retrieve suitable garments, I asked him to specify and was glad I did. I mistakenly thought he wanted me to bring my evening wear, but that was not at all what he meant.

'No, no, your most *expensive* articles of clothing,' he had said. 'Preferably something well worn.'

'I suppose that could be my late father's cashmere Scottish jacket—beautiful, in a soft green, which I haven't put on since last Christmas.'

'Does it smell of mothballs?'

'No. Mary aired it out last month. I wear it, as I said, at the holiday. But it might have a small hole or two.'

'Perfect! Get it, and your finest old city shoes as well. That bespoke pair you used to wear when I first met you.'

'What are we trying to convey, here, Holmes?'

'Respectability. Old money. Do it.'

'Why do you care?'

'I don't. It is a plan. Hurry, Watson.'

With our seasonal early sunset, it was dark and brisk as Holmes and I made our way on foot south from Baker Street to the Mayfair residence of the missing Reginald Weathering. The pavement was slick with ice, and despite the attentions of the street sweepers in this well-maintained enclave of extreme wealth, mounds of snow filled the gutter and clustered at the base of each building, appearing purple in the evening light.

The warm glow of gas and incandescent lighting threw

squares of gold light onto these mounds and the glistening pavement. As we passed holly-bedecked restaurant windows, I glimpsed elegant patrons toasting with silver filigreed mugs, others enjoying roast beef. No dusty, loud public houses here. There was a place to congregate for every taste and social class.

Soon we arrived at a six-storey building of graceful mansion flats in red brick, trimmed in bright white, with high, arched windows and small curved balconies. Such buildings had gone up all over London in recent years. With two flats per floor, and attended by a porter and housekeepers, they were designed to attract the wave of new young doctors, solicitors, and well-heeled university graduates, flocking to London to make their fortunes. Holmes pulled me into a narrow space between that building and the next. 'We shall wait here, Watson, until someone else is rung in. I do not want to give this couple the chance to bolt.'

As we waited, I mused that we looked casually wealthy, as best we could, being neither casual nor wealthy. Of course, Holmes was typically elegant in his sharply tailored frock coat and top hat. As he had reminded me earlier, many people considered detective work to be a rather lowly profession, which he mitigated, in part, by a certain sartorial flare. On the other hand, receiving prospective clients at 221B, he felt no compunction to impress. Rather, the opposite. I suppose it was this very lack of concern while at home that gave him a kind of upper hand with our visitors. Few failed to notice his house slippers.

There is a certain power in insouciance, I suppose.

In my pocket, at Holmes's request, was my Webley. And in his leather-gloved hand, an expensive holly wreath, laced with red and gold ribbons, purchased along the way. I similarly carried a costly bottle of port. It appeared as though we were on our way to a party.

A svelte young woman with a remarkable red hat, adorned with several stuffed birds and a flirtatious veil, approached the building with a key and unlocked the door. Holmes rushed forward and caught the door then rudely blocked her entrance.

'If you please, sir!' she cried.

'I asked you to stay away,' said Holmes.

The exquisitely attired lady raised her veil and . . . oh, how had I missed this when Holmes hadn't? It was Heffie, though quite transformed.

'Oh, Mr Holmes, really. I am Lady Emerald this evening,' said she in a voice that I would scarcely have recognized as Heffie's. She slipped past him into the well-lit foyer.

We followed her inside.

'That is a ridiculous pseudonym,' said Holmes.

Heffie reverted to her usual East End voice. 'I knows. But I likes it.' She smiled.

'Where did you get the key?' I asked, astonished.

She mimed picking a pocket.

'You cannot come with us, Heffie. I gave you a task the day before yesterday. Locating Mr Peter Findlay is a far more urgent mission.' said Holmes.

'I've already dunnit. Here's 'is 'ouse address.' She took a

small slip of paper from her reticule and handed it to Holmes, who glanced at it and pocketed it. 'Odd, though. 'E's working over at the docks. Ferrar and Sons Shipping. But something strange is up at 'is house. It's like a kind o' business.'

'How did you find where he lived?' I asked, stunned at her efficiency.

'I told 'em at Ferrar I were the new cleaner. Pulled out the employee records when they wasn't looking. Simple. Just took a mop and bucket and a stupid mob cap. Got to say, I prefer these duds,' said she, gesturing at her finery.

'Well done, Heffie!' I exclaimed.

'A business at his house? Are you sure it is where he lives?' asked Holmes.

''Course. I waited, saw him return there last night.'

'Remarkably thorough,' I said.

'It is why I employ her, Watson,' said Holmes. 'What kind of business?'

'Sign says "Baby Village". Twenty little ones in there. But nothing good of it. The girl running it is a holy terror. Those little ones need 'elp, Mr 'olmes. I ain't clear wot's going on in there.'

Was this woman perhaps selling children as well?

'Oh, an' one more thing. I 'ad a friend watch this 'ere 'ouse. This mysterious lady didn't go out all day yesterday, neither.'

'Well done, Heffie,' said Holmes, thinking. 'But you cannot come inside with us now.'

'Oh, dear sir, you remove all the amusement from my travails,' said 'Lady Emerald' in a cultured accent.

127

'That is too formal, Heffie. You'll give yourself away.'

'One must learn,' said she. I will admit that her accent had impressed me. 'By the way, the name of the prisoner is Katarina. It was engraved on a gift this Perkins feller had made.'

'We do not yet know that she is a prisoner,' said Holmes.

Heffie shrugged. 'Something ain't right.'

Holmes looked troubled. 'I agree. Heffie, I do not like this. There may be danger here.'

'No worries,' said the girl. 'I've 'elped you before, you know.' She paused, imploring him with a look. 'Please. I'd like to see this through.'

Holmes laughed. 'Oh, all right then. But stay well back. And speak very little. You are not quite passing.'

Moments later, we stood before the door to Reginald Weathering's flat. We rang.

'Who's there?' came a distinguished voice from within.

'Oh, it's Scott and Sanderson, old fellow,' drawled Holmes. He chuckled.

'And Lady Emerald,' Heffie added, in her polished voice. 'We have brought you a wreath.'

There was a long pause. I leaned in close to whisper.

'Wait, who am I, Holmes? Scott or—?'

'*Shh.*'

'What?' came the voice from inside.

'A wreath!' said Holmes. 'Is this George? George Perkins? You are having the party?'

The door was opened a crack. Facing us in an embroidered velvet smoking jacket and a matching smoker's hat with a tassel stood a short, well-fed man in his mid-thirties, with sleepy eyes and a profusion of dark, curly hair. He held a whisky in a crystal glass in one hand, a cigar protruding from two fingers.

His eyes flicked over the three of us. We must have passed some kind of muster, for he smiled. His teeth were white against his dark complexion. He was a remarkably handsome man.

'I am Perkins, yes, but there is no party,' he said.

'No party?' said Holmes. 'Miss Katarina said . . . Well, in any case, we have this wreath for you.' He thrust it at the narrow gap, and as Perkins opened the door to take it, Holmes inserted his foot over the threshold.

'She . . . How . . . ? I did not order any wreath!' exclaimed the man. Upon eyeing it, however, he relented. 'Although it is rather a nice one.'

'And it has a name on it,' said Holmes, shaking the wreath insistently. He was slurring his words slightly, as though well into his evening libations. '"George Perkins." That *is* you, isn't it? It must be a gift.'

Perkins reached out to take it. '*Ouch!*' The holly was sharp-edged. He started to close the door, but could not. 'Remove your foot, please.'

'I cannot, you have it wedged in the door,' said Holmes, with a rather silly grin. 'We are here for the party, old fellow.'

'I don't know any Sanderson or Scott. You must have the wrong flat,' said Perkins.

'But you are George Perkins? Five B? No, this is right.

129

*Ho ho!* It's nearly Christmas! I need some refreshment! That looks like an excellent Scotch you have in your hand there, my good man.' Holmes's voice had an almost manic gaiety quite unlike him. He was doing a credible impression of inebriation.

'I tell you, there is no party here. I have no idea how you—'

'Oh, bother!' Holmes turned to Heffie. 'Didn't you say Katarina invited us, darling?'

Heffie peeked past Holmes with a flirtatious smile at the valet. 'Indeed, my dear Mr Perkins, Kat-Kat invited us,' purred Heffie, as Lady Emerald. 'Yes. It was yesterday, at Worth's. She invited us *very particularly.*'

'Kat-Kat?'

'She is here, is she not?' Heffie smiled again. 'Katarina!' she called out.

'You could not have met her at Worth's,' said Perkins, still blocking us all at the door. 'She was in all day yesterday.'

'My dear sir, many women secretly visit Worth's,' said Heffie, with a sympathetic wink, 'and do not let their husbands know!'

'Oh, hell, may we not come in, my good man?' slurred Holmes. 'I have managed to prick my finger on this damnable holly—yes, even through my glove here—and I should like to wash the blood off my hand.'

'No!'

Holmes gave me a quick glance and nodded. I knew his signal at once. He signed one, two, three with the fingers of his hidden hand, and on three we both violently shoved the door. George Perkins stumbled back, dropping his whisky glass on the parquet floor where it shattered into a thousand diamonds swimming in gold liquid.

'Who are you? What do you want?' the fellow snarled as we charged through the door, Heffie on our heels.

I shut the door behind us. At the same time, I drew my Webley and turned to aim it at Perkins.

The man went white.

Heffie looked around in approval. 'A lovely abode, Mr Perkins,' said she, in that 'educated' voice.

Perkins backed slowly away from us, one hand raised, the other withdrawing a heavy gold pocket watch from his jacket. 'My watch. Here, please take my watch, and . . . and . . . this ring! And . . .' He started to reach towards his other pocket. 'Cash. I can give you cash.'

'Mr Perkins, hands where I can see them, please,' said Holmes. 'We are not here to rob you. However, we do have some questions. Answer them carefully or you will be with the police within the hour.'

Perkins froze. 'Police? I—I—'

'Let us all go into your sitting-room there and discuss this like reasonable gentlemen . . . and lady.' Holmes nodded towards next room. 'Depending on the outcome of this discussion, you will either go to prison or walk free.'

Moments later we faced Perkins in a richly appointed sitting-room where a fire burned brightly in the grate and glinted off polished brass fireplace implements. Silver candelabra illuminated the space in an inviting, warm light. Electric fixtures, I noted, were unlit, leaving the candles and fire to cast a warm glow. An orange cat slumbered on a hassock.

'Sit, Mr Perkins. Watson, stay with him.'

'But I only took two little things. And I bought . . .' stuttered the valet.

'Quiet,' said Holmes.

Perkins swallowed nervously and sat on a chair. I sat on a settee facing him, keeping the gun trained on him. A Christmas tree, glittering in ribbons and shiny baubles but with unlit candles, stood behind him. A garland of pine tied in silver bows was threaded across the fireplace mantel, winding past china figurines, cut crystal trinkets and a small plaster bust of, I assume, Venus. In the heat, the scent of freshly cut pine filled the room. It was not unpleasant.

'Watson! Eyes on the prize, if you would.'

The man leaped to his feet, glaring at me. 'Watson, is it?' he said. 'I suppose that is a false name, also?'

'Sit down, sir. Now,' I said.

I waved the gun at him, and Perkins slowly sank back onto the chair. He had transformed from a man of leisure into a cornered wild animal. He went very still, eyes riveted on the gun. I kept it trained on him.

To one side, Heffie moved to a table on which were a veritable clutter of very expensive and feminine knick-knacks. She began to examine them with dainty mews of appreciation. The orange cat suddenly mewed back. Heffie laughed.

'Heffie!' Holmes barked.

She stopped at once, with a quick grin behind Perkins' back. I did not think this appropriate, given the gravity of the situation. A man was missing, and as far as I imagined he might well have been murdered. And who knew whether the lady who had been seen in the window was a prisoner or not?

Perkins was certainly displaying all the indications of guilt. A bead of sweat ran down the fellow's face, and he flicked it away. 'Please . . . please, just tell me what you want. Whatever it is, you can have it . . .' he said at last. 'Whoever you are.'

'You have aroused suspicion, Mr Perkins. You have been seen in several costly establishments this past week, spending exorbitant amounts of money.'

'There is nothing criminal in spending money,' said Perkins. 'And I only took—'

'We are not here about petty theft. Spending that kind of money on a valet's salary is extraordinary. But you are also suspected of harbouring a young lady here. We understand you are not married?' said Holmes.

'That is none of your business.'

'Is the lady a prisoner? That, too, has come under question.'

'Ridiculous! Where do you come by this information? Have you been following me?'

'No, this lovely lady has.'

He whirled to face Heffie and eyed her with hostility. 'Impossible! I would have noticed.'

'Not likely, sir,' said Heffie.

'But perhaps one question supersedes them all,' continued Holmes. 'Where is Reginald Weathering?'

'Who . . . who are you?' stammered the man.

'My name is Sherlock Holmes, and this is my friend and colleague, Dr Watson. We have been engaged by the Marquis of Blandbury to find his son. At all costs.'

The man's eyes widened in utter panic. 'The Marquis? Sherlock Holmes! The detective? Dear God!'

There was a soft thump as George Perkins slid from his chair onto the floor in a dead faint.

# CHAPTER 14

## *The Lady in Question*

n a moment, I had Perkins on the settee and revived him with the smelling salts I routinely carried with me. He spluttered and sat up, staring in fear at Holmes.

'Now let us get to business, Perkins,' said my friend. 'Where is Reginald Weathering? You can either produce him, inform us reliably as to his whereabouts, or you can come with us to the police station. Now.'

The man swallowed. His eyes darted about. 'I can't. He has run off. Or rather, he moved out. He . . . left this flat to me.'

'*Hmm.*' Holmes nodded to me. 'The gentleman with me here is an undercover policeman. He does indeed have the authority to arrest you at this moment if you continue to lie to us.'

*Ah*, I was now a policeman. Impersonating an officer of the law held a certain risk. But I thought I could manage this role for a short time.

Perkins' eyes raked over me. He grew bolder. 'He is no policeman! A copper would never sit down. And that is far too nice a jacket.'

Holmes laughed. 'You know your tailoring, of course you do. You are a valet.'

The man said nothing.

'Unusual attire for yourself, though,' said Holmes.

The man stood. 'I am a private individual now.'

'That *is* a lovely smoking jacket,' remarked Heffie as Lady Emerald, approaching Perkins and stroking a velvet sleeve. 'I saw you buy it on Jermyn Street. Very, very costly, all that embroidery. And the matching little hat. Dashing.'

Perkins pulled away. 'Get out,' said he, staring hard at Heffie. 'You are a fraud. You are no Lady. That accent!' He looked at me. 'And you are not going to shoot me.' Finally, Perkins turned to Holmes. 'I don't even know if you *are* the real Sherlock Holmes. Perhaps all of you are lying. I am calling the authentic police!'

Holmes laughed. 'Indeed, I am Sherlock Holmes, and yes, please do call the *authentic* police.'

There was a pause.

'I did not think you would,' said Holmes. 'Where is Reginald Weathering? Produce him. And the lady who is now living with you.'

'Reginald is in Venice,' said Perkins. 'I am now the legal owner of this flat. He gave it to me. And he left me

136

considerable means as well. As for the lady—there is no lady here.'

'I have seen her,' said Heffie. 'In your window.'

'You are a little liar, madam,' said Perkins, with all the dignity he could muster in his ridiculous attire.

'She is no liar, Perkins, but she does work for the police. You will need some concrete evidence to dig yourself out of this hole. Watson, please summon a carriage. We will take this man to the station ourselves. I think the three of us can handle this squalling shrimp. It is time to search this flat.'

'How dare you!'

'Would you prefer to answer some questions instead?'

'I—I—Yes!'

'You promised Reginald's father that he would write to his parents. Why? His failure to do so is out of character. His parents are frantic with worry,' said Holmes.

'Frantic? I doubt that.'

'And the young lady? You say she is not here? We are advised that this young person has not left this flat in days. Is this lady a prisoner?'

'That is a ridiculous assumption. There is no lady!'

'And yet you responded to the mention of Katarina just now at your door. I will soon see about her. But one thing puzzles me most of all. Why would young Mr Weathering give this flat to you, his valet?'

'For services rendered,' said Perkins, through clenched teeth.

'And also . . . he is no longer a valet,' said a soft voice behind us.

We turned to see an elegant, slim woman standing in the doorway. At last, the mysterious Katarina.

And what a remarkable woman she was. She had a stunning, if slightly theatrical, beauty with a stylish pouf of spun gold hair, and was attired in a pink and maroon lace concoction that perfectly set off a tiny waist and her pale complexion. I noted that she sported a touch of rouge and colour on her lips, delicately and artfully applied. An actress, perhaps? She certainly had the graceful carriage of someone trained in ballet. A whiff of French perfume completed the altogether charming presentation.

I had known men to kill for less.

She smiled. 'As you can see, I am hardly a prisoner.' The ease of her bearing and the serenity of her expression gave credence to that statement.

Holmes said nothing but stared at the woman. There was a long silence.

'Let me clarify something,' said the vision before us. 'Lord Reginald Weathering has released Mr Perkins from service and has rewarded my darling handsomely for his long support.' She smiled. 'We are to be married.'

Her melodic voice had a slight husky quality. I could understand how Heffie, hearing her through the door, thought she might have been crying.

Holmes continued to stare at the woman. He was seldom without words, and in his silence I felt compelled to step in.

'We are satisfied that the lady is not a prisoner, but where has young Reginald gone?' I asked.

'Just a moment, Watson,' said Holmes. 'Mr Perkins, you have failed to introduce us to the future Mrs Perkins.' On his face was a certain smile that did not bode well for those who crossed him.

'Now you wish for social niceties!' cried Perkins. 'As she has told you, this lady is my . . . well, soon to be . . . wife. I present to you Miss Katarina Descanso.'

'And have you set a date for this wedding?' asked Holmes.

The couple exchanged a look. 'Not yet,' said the lady.

'Miss Descanso,' said Holmes, 'if you are no prisoner, why do you never leave this flat?'

The gentle lady drew back ever so slightly. 'Well, of course I do.'

'Not in three days. Not once. And you have refused to answer the door. We have had your flat watched and you have not stepped over the threshold.'

'Watched! Well, you shouldn't. That is none of your business. Who are you?'

'He claims to be the detective, Sherlock Holmes. But they are all liars,' said Perkins. 'Say nothing, my love!'

'I am most certainly Sherlock Holmes, and this is my colleague, Dr Watson. We are not the police, but if you are not careful you will both end up at the station. Miss Descanso, I suggest that you have chosen to remain within these walls because you are afraid. And, if I am not mistaken, you have every reason to be,' said Holmes.

She did not reply. The cat moved in close and leaned against her skirts.

'Come with me into the street just now, Miss Descanso.

Alone. I wish a word with you. There is a bright street-lamp just outside. We will stand so that you may all watch us.'

'Why would I do such a thing?'

'So that you can assure me, away from Mr Perkins here, of your free will, madam.'

Perkins leapt forward 'Absolutely not!' he cried.

'Stand back,' I commanded, raising the Webley once more. 'Sit over there.' I gestured to the settee.

'A gun!' exclaimed the lady. 'Oh, dear sir, you frighten us. Please!'

'How do I know you are not trying to abduct my darling?' cried the man. 'I demand to see some identification. Who knows if you are the real Sherlock Holmes? And . . . it's snowing outside. You can't just—'

'Sit down,' I repeated. 'Or I shall shoot you in the kneecap.' I would never do such a thing, but he did not know that.

'In my own house?' cried Perkins. He lunged at me. I aimed the gun into the air and caught him with my left hand, easily throwing him past me and onto the carpet where he landed with a loud grunt.

'*Ha!* Well done, Watson,' said Holmes. 'Mr Perkins, you overextend yourself.' To me, he added, 'Keep this gentleman, or so he would have us call him, occupied.' Holmes turned to the lady. 'Miss Descanso? A private word, if you please, if not outside, then in the hall.'

From the floor, Perkins rubbed the shoulder on which he'd landed and growled. The cat moved in close and leaned against her skirts.

'It is all right, George,' said the lady. 'I am not afraid.'

140

Holmes held out his hand to her.

She hesitated, but before she could object Holmes reached further, took up her hand and, to the lady's shock, raised it to his lips. He kissed her hand, then strangely turned it over, and then back again, studying it. Still keeping hold of this hand, he suddenly reached up with his other hand and gently stroked her face.

*What on earth?*

'Sir!' she said, attempting to pull free.

This impropriety was so unlike Holmes. It was as if he were somehow *entranced* by the lady.

He dropped her hand abruptly and stepped away from her. '*Ah*, but of course. It was the third of my theories. Remarkable. Mr Perkins, Miss Descanso, I fear you do not appreciate the danger of your situation. Both of you.'

Miss Descanso's demeanour shifted. She grew sombre, perhaps even frightened. She moved farther away, at more distance from Holmes, and patted her hair self-consciously.

There was a long silence. Perkins rose from the floor and stood uncertainly, looking from one of us to the other. Holmes did not take his eyes off Katarina Descanso.

I became aware of a longcase clock ticking in one corner. The fire crackled. I glanced at Heffie, who was staring wide-eyed at the scene.

George Perkins mustered his bravado. 'Who are you people?' He pointed at Heffie. 'This harridan is no lady. Do you take me for a fool? She has pocketed a small keepsake from our table.' Our eyes flew to Heffie, and she shrugged with an impish smile.

Holmes shook his head. 'Put it back, Heffie.'

She did. It was a small silver thimble. 'This feller lifted it from an antiques shop,' said she. 'I was going to return it.'

'Heffie?' Perkins cried. 'Not *Lady Emerald*?' Emboldened, he turned to me. 'And as I said, *you* are no policeman! I'll have you arrested for laying hands on me in my own home. And impersonating the law. And as for you, whoever *you* are—' He faced Holmes in a fury.

My friend stared back, unperturbed.

'Darling—' said Katarina gently, moving to Perkins' side and taking his arm.

But the little fellow's rage had seized hold of him. 'Who knows who you are?' He glared at Holmes. 'You spout a famous name but cannot prove it. I'll see you arrested for impersonating . . . for misrepresenting . . . for falsely . . .'

Holmes chuckled.

'George,' said Miss Descanso, softly. 'Darling.'

Perkins broke off, suddenly unsure. He glanced at the lady in confusion. He turned back to Holmes.

Holmes stared at the duo with a rueful smile. After a moment, he looked pointedly at the lady. 'Miss Descanso?'

The lady said nothing.

'Do you wish for your father to know?' said he.

*Know what?* I wondered.

'Absolutely not,' said the lady.

'I see. And regarding the deed to this flat? Have you actually signed it over to this man yet?'

'That is not your business,' said she.

'Please, just answer. I am trying to help you.'

'No. I have not signed it over.'

In retrospect, I am embarrassed that it was not until this moment that I fully ascertained the ruse. Katarina, of course, *was* Reginald Weathering! The possibility that young Reginald was impersonating a lady hadn't crossed my mind once I set eyes on the stunning Miss Descanso. Even now, I could scarcely believe it. This ethereal creature could not possibly be a man. The entire effect was so utterly feminine, it seemed impossible.

'Sir!' I blurted. 'Your disguise is so . . . so perfectly convincing!'

'It is not a disguise,' said the mysterious figure sharply. 'This is *who I am.*'

Heffie had moved to stand beside Holmes and me, staring at the beautiful woman before us in frank admiration.

'I seen this before,' said she, in her normal, East End voice. 'Round the town. In the theatre. But never as good as this. Cor, you 'ad even me fooled. 'Ow do you do that face colourin' so perfect, if you don't mind my askin'?'

Katarina smiled. 'I have friends in the theatre.' She turned back to us. 'It seems that no one in this room is who they appear to be. Even my dear George is . . . quite the gentleman, now.' She took his arm. 'But darling, you always were. And before that, you were the best valet a man could have. Mr Holmes—for you must *be* the real Sherlock Holmes—what gave me away?'

'Perkins here, when he was your valet, did he keep your clothes impeccable?' asked Holmes.

144

'Yes.'

'And did he do your expert barbering as well?' Holmes continued with a twinkle, stroking his own, clean-shaven cheek.

'Still does,' said Katarina, then gasped suddenly with the realization, stroking her own, delicate face. '*Ha ha!* Of course, it is now late in the day and my chin betrays me.'

'Precisely. I had my suspicion from the start,' said Holmes. 'However, I'll admit this was the last of three theories, and upon seeing you I required more proof. The effect is persuasive.'

The elegant person before us blushed.

Unlike the police, Holmes would never presume a theory was correct without immutable evidence. And no one was better at ferreting it out. I was filled with admiration for my friend.

George dropped his belligerent pose, took a step backwards and stared at us all in dismay. He removed his smoker's cap and twirled the tassel nervously.

'Now then,' said Holmes. 'At least I am satisfied that there has been no violence. But there has been harm done.' He turned to Katarina. 'You must rectify it. And here is what you must do, Miss Descanso.'

I marvelled at his ease with her new name. But I should not have.

'First of all, understand that your secret is safe with me,' continued Holmes. 'It is your business. However, if you intend to retain at all times the form in which I see you now—'

'It is not a form. Not a costume. Not a ruse. Truly, inside, Mr Holmes, I *am* this lady you see before you.'

'I believe you. Listen to me carefully. I will dictate to you a way out of this situation. If you are to escape prison, to escape the pursuit of your parents, you must do exactly as I say.'

'But—'

'You must. You have been thoughtless and inconsiderate. Your mother feared that you had been murdered or abducted, hence my involvement. You are fortunate that the Marquis did not bring in Scotland Yard, as the law would not treat you kindly. The police can be a danger to you, as can the general public.'

The couple looked at each other uneasily. They were surely aware of this. People had been arrested, gaoled, attacked in the streets for less. I had personally witnessed the brutal beating of two young men caught in women's clothing.

George Perkins took his love's hand in his, and the bond between them was evident. I could not take my eyes off the alluring Katarina. Beneath the delicate features and beautiful hair was a human being born a man. And yet there was something so utterly womanly in the person.

She took a deep breath. 'I am listening.'

Holmes then laid out his requirements. Katarina must, according to Holmes's stipulation, pay a visit to her parents *as Reginald*, to show that the son they loved was safe. 'Reginald' was to tell them that he had given the flat to the valet Perkins and was moving to the South of France.

Frequent letters to the parents going forward were part of the requirement. The flat was to be sold and George and Katarina must move elsewhere in the city without a forwarding address, so that Lord Weathering could not pay them an uninvited visit.

'He would surely know me,' Katarina had admitted. 'Even as you see me now.'

Once all had been agreed upon, Holmes picked up his hat which he had laid on a table near the door. 'I will confirm to the Marquis that I have seen you in person. If the truth comes out at a later date, I ask only that you declare that *I saw you in both incarnations, and as the lady you fooled me, too.*'

'But . . . you were not deceived,' said Katarina Descanso. Holmes did not reply.

A tear coursed down George Perkins' face. He wiped it away with a monogrammed handkerchief. 'Oh, my dear sir, thank you so much for not sharing our secret,' he said to Holmes. 'What a caring gentleman you are! And so open-minded.' He approached Holmes and in a sudden move enveloped my friend in a hug.

Holmes flinched, uncomfortable as always with physical contact. George did not let go. Holmes glanced over at me.

'We must be off, Holmes, we are late,' I said, and Perkins released him.

At the door, Holmes paused and turned back to the couple. 'Do not mistake me. I am utterly impartial here and your private life is your own. I was employed to find you, and to make certain no foul play had occurred. I am satisfied.'

'Then you don't approve of us, Mr Holmes? Not . . . just a little?' said the lady.

'Madam, I neither approve nor disapprove. Parents often want something different for their offspring, other than—' Holmes hesitated '—than what the child actually needs. Make this right with your mother, whose worry has caused her great pain. Good evening.'

He turned to go but paused. 'And put back the silver candle snuffer, Heffie. Unless Perkins here lifted that as well.'

''E did, but all right,' Heffie grinned, reached into a pocket and retrieved a second shiny object, setting it on a table.

'George, you must stop that!' Katarina retrieved the beautiful thing and handed it back to Heffie. 'Keep it, Lady Emerald,' said she, smiling. 'Snuff many candles in style. And Merry Christmas.'

Out in the street the snow drifted down once again. I looked up at the windows above us. High on the fifth floor I saw the pair we had just left, silhouetted and staring down at us. As I watched, Perkins put his arm around Katarina. They waved at us.

My feelings on this entire matter were conflicted. What I had been taught and what I now felt were at odds. Why should these two not seize happiness where they found it? Confused as I was, I knew that I had witnessed true love. I wished them the best. I waved back.

Heffie interrupted my thoughts. 'Well, Doc, I thought I'd

seen plenty, but I'll admit I didn't see that one coming, neither.'

I laughed. But when had Holmes known, exactly? Was it not until he stroked the lady's face? I turned to ask my friend, but saw his lone, thin figure disappearing up the street into the icy mist. 'Holmes!'

'Go on, now, Doc, and treat that overworked bloke to a good, stiff drink,' said Heffie. ''E could use it. Merry Christmas.'

'Merry Christmas, Heffie,' I said, then ran to catch up.

One mystery had been cleared, but in spite of our progress on the Endicott case, there was still a small child who remained in danger.

## CHAPTER 15

# *Baby Village*

he next morning, I awoke to discover a light blanket of snow had enveloped London, and once again Holmes had gone out early. I ate my breakfast alone, while contemplating the surprising conclusion to the Weathering case the night before.

It was, perhaps, the first time in my life that I had allowed into my thoughts any real understanding of the perils such men as Weathering and Perkins faced. I pondered how such very private choices could elicit violent hatred. Holmes's benignly neutral view made considerable sense to me.

As an unremarkable man myself, I had escaped the cruellest jibes as a youth and had rarely felt censure either at school or as an adult. But Holmes's incisive intelligence, his uncanny deductions, his social discomfort, not to mention his occasional lapse in modesty—perhaps I am being kind here—must have made him a target as a youth, and frankly sometimes still invited censure. My friend was an odd duck, and duck hunting was a favourite pastime of many.

I had learned more of Holmes's schoolboy challenges during the case I have recounted elsewhere as *Unquiet Spirits*. But as for the Weathering and Perkins duo, who are we, after all, to pass judgment on private matters which do no harm to the participants, or to others? Last night I had been struck once again by the remarkable kindness that Holmes, that most unsociable of men, harboured within.

Thanks once more to Pliny, I was dozing in my chair when my friend returned. I awoke with a start to discover that it was after two o'clock!

'Sleep on, Watson,' he said happily, 'I am for a quick rest myself, but be ready at five, dear friend. We venture to Aldgate for a visit to the Findlay residence tonight. Dress warmly.'

He was remarkably cheery for a man aiming to confront a violent criminal in his den. But then, of course, this was precisely the sort of Christmas gift that a man like Holmes relished. With my own blood racing, I had to admit that I felt the same.

Some three hours later we found ourselves bundled in layers of wool, I with my Webley, cold and heavy in my coat pocket, and Holmes with that familiar keen expression of a hound on the scent of his prey. After a long cab ride through snowy streets, which grew increasingly blackened with grime as we travelled eastwards, we alighted a block or two from our destination. We found ourselves on a dismal side street north of the London docks, very far from any holiday jollity, standing at the corner of a dreary mews.

Facing us was a row of sooty apartments, crammed together, with tattered washing frozen on the lines between them, torn curtains and battered window casings announcing the sad state of affairs. Muffled sounds of shouted arguments, and banging emerged down the deserted mews, and a single emaciated horse was tethered at one end, shivering piteously. Blackened snow partially covered a pile of refuse mounded near the entrance to the mews, dispersing an awful reek. We both drew our mufflers over our noses.

Three doors inside the mews we noticed a small sign, poorly hand-lettered and hanging at a tilt, proclaiming that 'Baby Village' was within. This must be Findlay's business.

'What have we here, then, Watson?' murmured Holmes. 'If indeed Findlay is engaged in trading in human beings, why would he announce its location with a sign?'

We drew close. The window was cracked with a small hole in it, and shreds of fabric stuffing hung from the hole. Through it we could hear a female voice shouting, 'Get down! Get away! Ye little pack 'o wolves!'

Through the grime, we could make out the foggy shapes of two women and some small children moving about the room. Holmes took his handkerchief and rubbed away a small patch of frost and dirt from the glass for a better look inside.

A young, thin blonde woman came into sharper view, holding a swaddled infant in her left arm while distributing half-filled bottles of milk to three toddlers clambering at her legs. Clarice Findlay, I surmised. She looked barely nineteen, though it was hard to tell. Poverty and life on the edge had taken a severe toll. A cheap, grey wool dress hung on her thin frame, a grimy pink shawl around her bony shoulders. Her face was careworn and pale, her mouth drawn back in a grimace of effort. She looked, to my medical eye, like someone suffering from chronic pain. Indeed, her half-closed lids hinted at serious medication. I was quite certain that she was drugged.

Around the room were perhaps twelve or thirteen small children ranging in age from mere weeks to perhaps three or four years old. On a large, dirty mattress resting on the floor lay four infants, swaddled and sleeping, their tiny mouths open and drooling. A fifth had escaped his swaddling and thrashed dangerously close to the mattress's edge.

A second woman, old and equally tattered, moved to this little group and brusquely shoved the active infant back from the brink. It made no objection, no noise, no reaction.

Another infant in her arms lay limply, its head lolling back. Something was terribly wrong.

'Dear God, Holmes, those infants are drugged.'

Other slightly older children, seeing the bottles going to the infants, started up a chorus of shouting. They crowded around the younger woman, hands reaching up. Mrs Findlay handed a bottle to one child, who was really too young to hold it, and he dropped it immediately.

'Ye stupid git!' The older woman screamed, moved in and kicked the bottle across the floor.

The child who had let it go sat heavily on the ground, wailing. Two others near him took up the cry. An older child, perhaps four years old, scooped up the errant bottle and hungrily sucked at it, an empty bottle in his other hand.

'Stop! You already had yours!' shouted the older woman.

Moving to a counter behind this melee, Clarice Findlay took up an iron pan of milk which had been heating over a makeshift single burner. She poured the scalding liquid into a row of waiting bottles, then set down the pan and picked up a medicine bottle. With an eyedropper, she doled out a random splash of the medicine into each of the bottles.

'Laudanum,' murmured Holmes.

'Yes,' I replied. 'Far, far too much for an infant. A baby-minding service, do you suppose?'

'Of a sort,' said Holmes.

There were too many children, chaos, and not enough adults looking after them. One would have to be truly desperate to leave one's child here, I thought.

Capping each bottle, the older woman began distributing them, propping up the smaller babies with rough pillows. This was not terribly effective, and she and Mrs Findlay ran about the room, reinserting bottles into babies' mouths, some of whom responded by grasping the bottle. Others lay there, passive and glassy-eyed, the bottles tumbling from their lips.

As we watched, the noise level subsided and in a matter of minutes, every child in the room was asleep.

'Into the arms of Morpheus,' I said. 'Dear God.'

I felt a tap on my arm and turned to face a bedraggled girl, perhaps fourteen or fifteen, ghostly white, with deep purple shadows under her eyes. Clothed in layers of rags, she had one thin red handkerchief pinned to her hat, folded into a makeshift flower at an attempt at gaiety. The snow, which had begun falling again, drifted down, dusting her hat and shoulders. She had a paper in her hand and waved at me. 'Pardon me, sir, I'm lookin' for Baby Village,' said she. 'But this 'ere looks like a . . . a house.'

'It is here,' said Holmes sharply, with a quick glance at the girl.

It was then that I noticed a tiny infant, swaddled in rags, held tight to her chest.

'You are here to leave your child?' I asked. She was barely more than a child herself.

'Yes. My first time. Is this the place?'

'Er, yes,' I said.

'Please. I cannot be late to work.'

Baby Village, then, was a service for minding the children of factory workers. It was five in the afternoon, and already dark. The girl must work nights.

'Miss, you really should not leave your infant here,' I said.

'That way. That door there,' said Holmes sharply. As she started to pass us, he asked, 'Do you mind telling me how much you pay to leave your little one?'

'Thruppence a day,' said the girl meekly. 'I s'pose there's cheaper but I ain't got no time to look. Ezekial here, he came two weeks early and I—' She slipped on the ice, and I caught her and her newborn infant.

'Let me help,' I said. She looked up blearily at me and seemed at last to take in the notion that neither I nor Holmes fitted in with the neighbourhood.

'You ain't the police?' She looked suddenly frightened. "Cause I ain't done nothing wrong.'

'We are not policemen,' said Holmes in a soothing tone. 'This gentleman is a medical doctor. We have been called to check on the health of the babies here.'

Relief washed over her features. 'Good,' she said. 'They are looked after, then.'

Holmes and I exchanged a glance. Without warning, she thrust the infant into my arms and then dashed away, calling over her shoulder, 'Tell 'er I'll pay when I pick him up.'

'But what is your name?' I cried.

'Sally O'Rourke' she called and was gone.

Holmes stared down at the tiny baby in surprise.

'Just like that,' I said. 'Giving her infant to a stranger!'

'Of course, you do look trustworthy, Watson,' said Holmes. 'I have always said so.'

'Let's get this child inside.'

The door was unlocked and, in a moment, we faced the exhausted young woman. She glanced at the infant in my arms and shook her head, refusing us entry.

'Mrs Findlay?' inquired Holmes.

'Yes. But I can't take on no more wee 'uns,' she said harshly. 'An' 'oo are you, anyways? You don't need my services, lookit the two o' you.'

'I've come to talk to you, Mrs Findlay. About your time at the Marylebone Workhouse,' said Holmes.

It was fortunate that the young woman did not have a babe in her arms, so shocked was she by my friend's words. She reeled back and started to close the door. Holmes blocked it with his hand.

'Go away!' she cried. 'Do not talk to me about that place. I . . . I . . . never been there.'

'I think you have.'

Tears came unbidden but with them flared an instant rage. '*Go away*, or I'll call the police!' she shouted, pushing hard on the door.

'No, you won't, Mrs Findlay. Your business here will not stand the scrutiny.'

Behind her, the other woman looked panicked. 'Clarice, make them go!' she cried out.

Clarice glanced back. 'The flame, Martha!'

A rag near the makeshift burner had suddenly caught fire. The woman shrieked, then flung it into a pot of dirty water full of used bottles.

Clarice turned back to face us.

It struck me that we had more urgent business than to discuss Christopher. The snow was coming down as we stood on the doorstep, and the newborn in my arms was swaddled only in a single, thin blanket.

'This infant was dropped off by a young woman who

said she came to an arrangement with you. Sally O'Rourke,' I said. I held out the baby to her, feeling awful doing so.

She shook her head, refusing to take him. 'Give me the money,' she said. 'Five pence.'

'Let us in and we will pay you,' said Holmes. She let us through the door and Holmes fished in his pockets. 'The mother said three,' he said, and I gasped at his attempt to bargain.

''Price just went up,' said Clarice, folding her arms. Her eyes shone with a drug-induced bravado. It was on the sharp edge of madness, I thought. Holmes handed her the money.

'Martha!' barked Clarice. 'Take the little mouse.'

The older woman, having put out the flame, limped over to us and reached for the baby. As she did so, I got a whiff of sour milk and cheap gin, and I noted in her coarse features the distinctive look of a chronic alcoholic. I held onto the infant just a little too long, and she wrenched the newborn roughly from my grasp.

The woman called Martha then leaned down and scooped up a half-filled bottle lying next to a baby on the mattress and thrust it into this new child's mouth. The tiny baby, startled by the rough contact, turned his head away.

The older woman hissed in anger. 'I tol' ya, take no more in, Clarice. Lookit this'n. Won't take the bottle!' She thrust the newborn into Clarice Findlay's hands. ''E's all yours. I quit,' she said. 'But you owes me, Clarice, and if you don't pay, I'll send Roger an' 'is bruvver over 'ere and you'll be sorry. I've had enough.' She began to untie her apron.

'Martha, no!' cried Clarice. 'Please!'

Martha eyed us up and down. 'Lookit these two. They'll bail you out.'

'How much does she owe you?' asked Holmes of the older woman.

'Ten bob,' said Martha.

Holmes dug deep in his pocket, found ten shillings and extended his hand with the money. The woman attempted to grab it, but Holmes pulled his hand back. 'Will you stay on with Mrs Findlay if I pay you?'

'Martha, please,' whispered the younger woman.

Martha hesitated. Then, with a quick nod, she took the money from Holmes and retied her apron. She pulled the new arrival from Clarice Findlay's arms and took him away.

'Madam,' said Holmes to the bereft creature now standing before us, 'I need a word with you privately.'

'Now look what you done!' she moaned, as if the added child was somehow our fault. 'What do you want of me? How do you know my name? Martha will leave me, soon's you go, and I have all these needy little—oh, heaven help me!' She looked about wildly. Spotting the bottle of laudanum she had used in the children's bottles, she reached out towards it and—

Holmes grabbed her hand. She jerked her arm back as if burned, but he held on. 'Mrs Findlay, calm yourself. I am here to understand something that I think may have happened to you and your husband some years ago at the Marylebone Workhouse. I need you to clear something up for me.'

Her eyes widened with fear. 'Who are you?' she said.

The pupils were dilated and almost entirely blacking out the irises. Her eyes darted back to the laudanum. 'I just need a little—' Her free hand snaked towards the bottle, and Holmes caught it and held on.

'Watson, dispose of that.' He indicated the laudanum. I quickly poured it into the sink.

'Nooooo!' the young woman wailed.

'Is there somewhere we can speak alone?' asked Holmes. 'Tell Martha to take over for a moment—oh, no—that child! Watson!'

I followed his gaze to the dirty mattress where once again the same squirming infant was in danger of rolling off onto the filthy hard floor. I scooped the baby up and placed him in the centre of the mattress between two others, who appeared drugged into oblivion.

Holmes took Mrs Findlay by the arm and led her to the next room. I followed, and with one admonishing glance at Martha, shut the door behind us.

The adjoining room was little more than a dank closet with one high window looking out onto snow spattering down against a stained brick wall. A filthy mop, some shelves of scummy bottles, a box of some kind of milk powder, a row of medicines and a stool were all that was in view. No food. No toys. No creature comforts. A hypo-dermic syringe lay on one of the shelves.

The young woman wrenched free of Holmes's grip and stared at us defiantly. 'Who are you? What do you *want*?'

'You are married to Mr Peter Findlay, are you not?' asked Holmes.

'What if I am?'

'Mr Findlay claims to be the father of a little boy who was stolen from the two of you at the Marylebone Workhouse nearly four years ago, at this time of year.'

The woman blanched, swayed, and I caught her as she fell. I lowered her onto a short wooden stool and bent down close to support her. She groaned and leaned against me. She was so thin as to be nearly weightless. I gently pulled up her shawl which had slipped from her shoulders and wrapped it around her.

'I had a little boy. He . . . was not stolen. He . . . he died.'

'I see. My condolences. And has it been like this for you ever since?' Holmes asked.

'Like what?'

'The drugs.'

'I don't drug the babies.'

'You do. But that is not what I am asking.'

Clarice Findlay grimaced. 'I take care of the little ones. *Take care* of 'em. Because no one will take care of 'em if I don't. You see, I . . . I . . .'

'You are addicted to laudanum, Mrs Findlay. You cannot deny it.'

With a sudden wild strength, Mrs Findlay hurled herself to her feet.

'Get out. You're not police! You have no rights. Leave me alone!'

'Mrs Findlay, I have just one question. Your own baby? Did you see him before he . . . before he . . . left you?'

'My baby. See him? I held him in my arms!'

'Christopher?'

'Yes.' Her face lit up with the memory, and she paused and looked away, suddenly transported. The cold light from the small window highlighted her pale, almost translucent face. 'Born Christmas Day . . .' she said dreamily.

Holmes paused. Then, 'Did Christopher have a mark, dark red, on the back of his neck? A star?' he asked.

She turned to him in wonder. She nodded. 'The Star of Bethlehem, we called it.' She began to sob.

Nothing Holmes or I could say would stop her.

We left her weeping in the arms of her assistant and ran out into the snow like two thieves. Leaving behind those poor infants, I have never felt more villainous in the pursuit of justice.

I just hoped that Holmes had a plan of some sort. We could not let this rest.

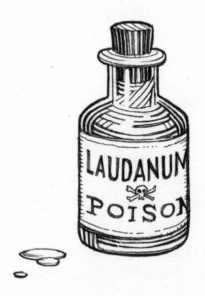

# CHAPTER 16

## A Father's Lament

olmes did not disappoint me.

As we waited at the entrance to the mews for the return of Peter Findlay, he confounded me by turning his back to the street, quickly applying a black moustache and donning gold-rimmed spectacles. A subtle adjustment to his hair, and the effect was complete. It was no longer Sherlock Holmes standing beside me!

At my puzzled look, he said, 'Findlay is due home at any moment. We have business to discuss, but I don't want him recognizing the man who nearly took him in Oxford Street. At least, not before we have him in our clutches. Look, there is our man now!'

The tall, muscular figure of the man known as Peter Findlay moved slowly down the street towards us. His posture reflected a kind of resolute despair. As he drew closer, I noticed the pale blue eyes I'd seen in Oxford Street and the scar over the right eyebrow that Holmes had described.

Just as Findlay was about to turn into the mews, Holmes stepped in front of him, blocking his way.

'Peter Findlay!' Holmes exclaimed with a broad smile.

The man paused. ''S'right. Do I know you?' he said gruffly. Liverpool, I thought, or thereabouts.

'I met you at Ferrar Shipping,' said Holmes, a trace of Lancashire in his voice. I had not heard him speak with a northern accent before. 'Someone told me to find you in the vicinity. I am in luck, and so, dear sir, are you! My name is Berenford Wallace, my company are shipbuilders out of Liverpool, and we are looking for some apprentice engineers. I have a proposition for you, sir. Are you familiar with the Liverpool shipping industry?' Holmes was remarkably fast on his feet.

'Indeed, I am, sir. I—I come from there.'

'May I stand you a drink, with my colleague here, Mr Ames?'

That was an offer the man would not refuse.

At the Wellford Arms, a rough and dingy public house not two streets away, Holmes bought a round, then sat us down at a stained wooden table in a corner niche. He proceeded to order drink after drink, downing them each in single gulp, matching Peter Findlay glass for glass.

While I am a man who can normally stand a few drinks

without effect, what transpired here was beyond my ability. I did not know until this moment that Holmes could hold his alcohol better than any man I'd seen in my life. It should not have surprised me. He was full of hidden talents.

Soon, they began trading maritime engineering stories and Holmes gave me the cue. 'Mr Ames here can't hold his liquor. Look, he'll be asleep in a minute. Won't you, Ames?'

I duly pretended to lapse into sleep with an occasional eye cracked to witness the following developments.

As the drinks continued to flow, Peter Findlay admitted he was less than eager to return home. At Holmes's urging, the man poured out his life story. He had been born into middle-class comfort, had success in school, and had even been taken on as an engineering protégé by a noted designer of steamships. But then his good fortune ended.

When Findlay was sixteen, his father was killed in a freak accident on the docks. The family income dropped to zero. 'We were on the streets in three months,' he revealed. His mother became an alcoholic, seemingly overnight.

He was given charge of his younger siblings, but one brother was 'not right in the head' and caused the family undue strain, even as Peter Findlay was forced to take an exhausting, menial job. 'The money was better, but not enough to support six people.' Then the brother in question got into a drunken brawl, killed a man, and went to gaol.

Findlay, by then well into his cups, admitted that he had abandoned his family, leaving their plight to the next older sibling, and ran off and 'married a beautiful young girl'. They moved to London, where he'd hoped to catch another engineering apprenticeship opportunity. My eye cracked open and I watched him as he sighed, looking off into the distant past. 'But I had my Clarice. She had bewitched me.'

'Women, they do that,' said Holmes sympathetically. 'You are still married?'

'I am. She . . . she has had her problems, poor soul. And luck was not with us. I got a good job, lost it, and then, through a series of misfortunes, we were forced to the workhouse.'

'But you are able to care for her now?' asked Holmes.

'I won't abandon my family again,' said Findlay defensively. 'No, sir. Not ever. I could not live with it.'

'My wife, too, had her problems, may she rest in peace,' said Holmes.

'She's dead then?'

'Laudanum,' said Holmes. 'Dangerous stuff, that.'

He was veering close to the edge here. I peeked again. I thought I discerned a slight suspicion dawning on Peter Findlay.

'But your wife? At least she is still alive?' said Holmes quickly.

Findlay nodded and swiftly wiped away a tear. He downed his fourth whisky and lapsed into a morose silence.

Holmes then matched Findlay's tale with a concocted story of his own, weaving a fiction so convincing I wondered if parts of it were not true. He described falling in love with a fragile young woman who became pregnant with their child. He subsequently lost his job, and they were

168

forced for a time into the workhouse. As I listened, I smiled inwardly at the many times he'd chided me for what he called embroidering the accounts of his cases.

At the mention of the workhouse, I heard a noise and cracked one eye to see Finley sit upright. 'What happened to them?' asked the man, suddenly animated. 'Your wife and child?'

'Look, Ames is awake now,' said Holmes, and I sat up and rubbed my eyes sleepily. 'Our child was taken from us, as they do,' he continued.

'As they do . . .' said Findlay bitterly.

'And my wife could not stand it. She ran away from the workhouse, and I never saw her again,' said Holmes.

'And the child?'

Here Holmes's voice grew very soft. 'That is the thing. I do not know. I just do not know.'

Peter Findlay's face went dark and he finished his drink in a single gulp. His eyes filled with tears. 'I was in the workhouse, and my wife gave birth to a child there. We called him Christopher. Born on Christmas Day. He had a birthmark on his neck in the shape of a star. The Star o' Bethlehem, we called it.'

Holmes and I stayed silent. After a moment Findlay went on.

'We lost our little boy. At least, I thought we did. They told us he'd died. My wife was fragile before we had our child, but Christopher's death sent her over the edge. She thought it was her fault. Even though I was able to move us out of the workhouse, she . . . she . . . suffered, and

169

she began to lose her faculties. *But I found a way to help her.*'

'How?' asked Holmes eagerly.

'I saved a little from my pay each week. I put it away. Carefully, so she would not know. And then I set her up in business.'

'What kind of business?'

'Child minding. To heal her mind. If she could care for other infants, I thought, perhaps it may be her salvation.'

That is not, however, what Holmes and I had witnessed. Holmes said nothing, letting Findlay continue. Surely the man knew what was going on at his wife's business? This could not have been what he intended.

Findley's eyes wandered back and forth. Holmes called for another round. It arrived and our guest tossed his back and took a deep breath.

'The business, has that helped her?' Holmes asked gently.

There was a long pause in which Findlay seemed to turn inward, as if we and all around him had vanished and he was utterly alone with his thoughts.

At last, he looked up. 'It is not . . . not working well. But I have another hope. There is another thing . . . no, I dare not say. But if I can succeed, I can pull my Clarice back from the brink.' He paused, looking around himself suspiciously, then leaned forward to Holmes and whispered, 'I have discovered that my boy is still alive. Clarice did not cause his death after all!'

'How do you know?'

Peter Findley reached into his threadbare jacket and

removed a tattered newspaper clipping. He spread it on the table before Holmes. I could see without examining it that it was the article detailing Mrs Huron's trial and the 'stolen orphans'.

There was a pause. Holmes nodded. 'I might be able to help you,' said he.

I could barely conceal my astonishment. Surely Holmes could not contemplate returning Jonathan back to the colossal wreckage of this father and mother? And yet that is precisely what the courts might do if we interfered.

'You don't know what I'm thinking,' said Findlay.

Holmes smiled. '*Ah*, but I do.' He peeled off his moustache and removed his glasses. He sat up, eyes clear and posture erect. His voice changed back to his own. 'You are thinking of a new way to get little Christopher back from the Endicotts.'

Peter Findlay staggered to his feet, knocking the chair over backwards. 'Who are you?' he shouted, outrage cutting through the layers of alcohol. He squinted at Holmes, who sat calmly before him, now in his own persona. A slow realization came over the man. 'I . . . I know you. You were in Oxford Street.'

'That is correct,' said Holmes. 'Did you even consider for a moment the child's safety as you planned to run through crowds on the ice like that, Mr. Findlay?'

Findlay wavered. 'I . . . I had to escape. I had to—'

'Sit down. This does not excuse you. I am sympathetic to your desire to help your wife, but your violence weighs against you.'

'*Who are you?*'

'Do as I say, or you will be in gaol before the hour is out. Sit!'

The man reluctantly took his seat again.

'Now, listen to me. My name is Sherlock Holmes. I am a private individual but closely affiliated with the law. I will help you, but only if you cooperate.'

'Help me? How?'

'There are conditions. The first is that you must close down your wife's business. She is endangering the babies under her care. I am sure you are aware of this.'

'But I hired her a helper. Clarice will improve, I know she will.'

'She will not without help. Today must be the last day of operation. Close Baby Village tonight, or I will see your wife in prison.'

'You don't understand. Christopher is *our child*. On Oxford Street, I saw the star, the star on his neck. Christopher! *He is our child!*'

'And you would take this child back? You are struggling to keep your current position. Alcohol has you in its grip. Your wife is addicted to laudanum.'

'We can do better. We can—'

'Look at yourself, man. Even if you prove your parentage, the courts will rule against you.'

*But we could not be sure of that*, I thought.

Findlay dissolved into tears. Despite his violence, his story was tragic, and I felt some degree of sympathy for the man. His bad fortune was not his fault. He was truly a victim of circumstance, providing he was telling the truth. Instinct told me that he was.

Holmes pulled out his notebook and from it removed a paper and a business card.

'I ought to have you arrested, Peter Findlay,' said he. 'Go home now. As soon as all the babies have been collected by their mothers, close up Baby Village, remove the sign from the window and never take in another child . . . ever.'

'My wife! Clarice will go mad.'

'Better that than other people's children die through your wife's negligence. Replace the sign with a new one announcing it is closed, then you must both pack up your belongings tonight and go to this address. Ask for Agnes. She will tell you what to do. You must complete all this by dawn, or the offer is off, and I'll see you both go to gaol.'

'But what of the poor mothers who leave their children? They rely on us.'

'Focus on your own problems. If you do not shut down this business, a child will die at your wife's hands. As little Christopher nearly did.'

'What do you mean? She would never harm our child.'

'Perhaps not intentionally. But the prison matron did find your Christopher lying on the cold cement floor next to your wife, who was insensible from opium. Claudine Huron rescued your son from near death. And she made sure it would never happen again.'

The look on Peter Findlay's face told us everything. Holmes had spoken the truth and the man knew it.

'Have you never loved a child?' cried Findlay between sobs. 'Our lives have been a living hell. Not a day goes by that we don't mourn Christopher. And then when I found out where he was . . . Well, what would you have done?'

'Not what you did.' Holmes's face hardened. 'You are a criminal. You knocked a woman down in the street. You broke into a home. You struck a man. You struck me, earlier. You threw a pot of boiling water at a young maid! And you attempted to abduct a young child from the only home he has known. Imagine the boy's terror, his distress.'

'The last thing I wish is to harm my little boy.'

'That is not good enough, Mr Findlay. I have sympathy for your longing, but none at all for your actions. I have anticipated your story, or much of it, and I have arranged help for you and Mrs Findlay.'

'Help?'

Holmes tapped the piece of paper he had set in front of Findlay.

'On this paper is an address. Be there *by dawn*. I will know whether or not you comply. And I reiterate—fail to do this and you will both be incarcerated. With what this gentleman and I saw today of your wife's conduct, she will not be free in a very long time. Make your choice.'

He handed the slip of paper to Peter Findlay.

'Now, go.'

In a hansom cab a few minutes later, I turned to see my friend lost in dark thoughts.

'I presume that you have set into motion some kind of plan, Holmes. May I know what it is?'

'Presume nothing, Watson. Presumptions lead to gross error.'

'But what have you done? Where have you sent the Findlays?'

Holmes closed his eyes. 'I am very tired, Watson. I have sent them to a place of last resort. This morning I made all the arrangements. In order for my plan to work, many things . . . so many things must . . . *Oh*, let it go, Watson. I need to think.'

He closed his eyes and would say no more.

# PART FIVE

## PEACE ON EARTH

*'True glory consists in doing what deserves to be written,*
*in writing what deserves to be read,*
*and in so living as to make the world happier*
*and better for our living in it.'*
—Pliny the Elder

# CHAPTER 17

## *Watson Gives Up*

wo days passed and Holmes came and went a number of times but remained silent and would not share any confidences. As the holiday spirit intensified outside our doors, it had grown ever more sombre at 221B, despite Mrs Hudson's efforts to infuse cheer. The fruit in our basket dwindled, with Holmes pressing some upon every delivery man and policeman who ventured across our threshold.

Holmes seemed deeply preoccupied and even disturbed. One evening, as I closed my book and was about to retire, he appeared at the door, dishevelled and irritated.

'Half of London seems to be taking a holiday, even the police,' he complained.

'It *is* Christmastime, Holmes.'

'Crime never ceases!' he snapped. Retreating into his

bedroom, he shut the door with a bang. I had known, of course, that Holmes was not one for celebrating the holidays, but his prolonged absences and ill temper had begun to wear on me. Why welcome me as a guest and then disappear for long stretches? Of course, that had always been my life with Holmes.

I remained in Baker Street for a day or two longer in the hope that I'd be further engaged on this case, but it was not to be. I finished the Pliny, and in a mischievous kind of revenge, I managed to place some pine boughs about the place, lending a pleasant aroma to the sitting-room. But I found them the next morning tossed in the grate.

I considered decamping early to my own home and was attempting to come up with an excuse but was spared that when, on the twenty-first of December, I received a letter from Mary informing me that she had finished early in Chester and would arrive home that very evening, some two days in advance of her plans. I left Holmes a note and returned at once to Paddington and my dear wife.

I will admit, however, to a nagging feeling of unfinished business.

On the following day, Mary distracted me with her good spirits and plans for our own private celebration of the holiday. I suggested inviting Holmes for Christmas dinner, to which Mary heartily agreed. I sent a note but received no reply.

On the twenty-third, I returned after lunch to my surgery, planning to close early, and proceeded through the small waiting area to my examination room. I was surprised to find Holmes seated there, perched on the end of my examining table, lost in thought.

He looked up, startled. 'Watson, at last.'

He was pale, as usual, and perhaps had grown even thinner in just the last few days. He was hardly a man enjoying the holidays, as most of London seemed to be doing.

'Are you well, Holmes?' I inquired. 'You look tired.'

'I am not here for medical advice, Watson. Are you free tomorrow evening at four p.m.?'

'On Christmas Eve?'

'Yes. The Endicotts' party for little Jonathan's birthday. It promises to be interesting. I may need your help.'

'My help? What has happened with that case? I have been eager to hear, Holmes.'

'I am sorry to have left you hanging. The danger to that child is perhaps lessened, but it is not entirely at rest. Your presence would be a great boon to me, dear friend.'

'What has become of the unfortunate Peter Findlay and that poor young woman? Are you expecting trouble at this party? And if there is danger, wouldn't it be a good idea at this point to involve the police?' I asked, wondering if Findlay had slipped from view and perhaps presented a renewed threat. At the thought, I was both worried and slightly upset not to have been involved.

'I have wrestled with my conscience on this matter, Watson. But I believe that what I have planned is the right thing, although it is risky. Will you join me?'

'I am sorry, Holmes,' I said, with genuine regret. 'Mary has committed us to a dinner that evening with our young neighbours, who have no family nearby.'

Holmes's look of disappointment struck me. But he quickly hopped off the table and made for the front door. 'Do not trouble yourself, Watson,' said he. 'I will manage.'

There was something afoot, and I knew him well enough to see it. 'Holmes?'

He turned back to me, and with an expression I could not read said simply, 'If anything changes, Watson, and you find you are able to come, be sure to—oh, never mind.'

'Be sure to what?'

'Bring your Webley, would you?'

'To a child's birthday party?'

He smiled.

'On Christmas Eve?' I persisted.

He shrugged, still smiling, and departed.

Neighbours' dinner or not, I would find a way to join him. As of course he knew I would.

# CHAPTER 18

## O *Tannenbaum!*

herlock Holmes has accused me of overly dramatizing my accounts for the reader by the way I have chosen to reveal his surprising deductions. But Holmes frequently withheld his theories from me, even as we confronted grave danger. For example, he deduced in advance, but did not identify to me, the serious threats we faced in stories I have recounted as 'The Speckled Band' and 'The Red Headed League'.

Whatever his reasons—and his love of the theatrical was part of it—it was not something that he was likely to change.

Therefore, on Christmas Eve, at four in the afternoon, we departed in our finest dress clothes for the Endicotts' party, with me none the wiser as to his preparations or his plans for this event. All I knew was that he wanted me with him, armed with a gun. As our cab headed south, I sat next to him, that old feeling of excitement coursing through my veins. The thrill of adventure was more piquant than any goose dinner. Thank the heavens I was blessed with a wife who understood me.

At last, we pulled up before the Endicotts' grand Mayfair house. The overcast sky was dark and a light snow had begun to fall. A row of beribboned lanterns had been set, leading to the entrance, and the door stood open to receive guests, the cheery warm light spilling onto the portico.

My thoughts were churning as we descended from our cab.

Two servants in festive red velvet greeted the arriving guests, checking each name against a list. My tension rose as we awaited our turn, but I knew that questioning Holmes further would lead nowhere. We were soon greeted and sent inside. There seemed to be more footmen on hand than one might expect. Guards of some sort, perhaps?

One more approval was needed, a careful once-over by the formidable butler, Jones. 'Mr Holmes and Dr Watson,' said the man with an icy formality. His sudden reserve was alarming, given his previous enthusiasm towards my friend. 'That way,' he said, indicating a long hall to our left, where the cheerful sounds of a small but refined crowd drifted out.

As we approached that room, I wondered at the butler's chilly response. 'What was that about?' I asked.

'Jones is not happy about this situation. I believe he advised cancelling this party.'

'Then I conclude you have informed the Endicotts that the man who has threatened them believes himself to be the rightful father.'

'I have. And I could see by Endicott's reaction that he knew it. Those letters.'

'He admitted as much to his wife?'

'No. I think he is ashamed not to have taken action.'

We were handed glasses of champagne and proceeded down the hall. Holmes put his glass down on a table and nodded for me to do the same.

Lady Endicott approached, beautifully attired in an elegant, forest-green silk dress. But her smile was strained. 'Gentlemen, we are pleased that you have joined us, though your plan is utterly opaque to me, Mr Holmes.'

'All will be well, Lady Endicott,' said Holmes reassuringly.

She smiled stiffly and moved away.

Holmes then glanced at me uneasily. 'While I expect the best, we must nevertheless be prepared for the worst, Watson. Keep your wits about you.'

'Why would I not, Holmes?' I said, setting my own glass down next to his.

We followed Lady Endicott into the Great Room, and there I was astounded. It was something from a storybook. An enormous Christmas tree, the likes of which I had never seen in a private home, filled a quarter of the room. It stood over sixteen feet tall, more than fourteen feet wide at the base and sparkled with glittering glass baubles, candies and small toys. It was adorned with a multitude of blazing wax candles. The heat from these caused the scent of pine to fill the room, overpowering the mulled wine, the ladies' perfume, the clove-studded oranges resting in silver bowls . . . overpowering all.

Underneath the tree lay a profusion of wrapped presents and set around these was a kind of barricade of red ribbons strung between several chairs.

Standing just outside these ribbons were a dozen or more children ranging in age from toddler to perhaps eleven or twelve. More scampered in from behind us. All eyes were transfixed upon the pile of gifts and the glittering tree. The children crowded in towards it, pointing and whispering. A tall young woman, perhaps a governess, kept watch and gently admonished one child who leaned into the ribbon.

'Be patient, Charles,' said she. 'Good things come to those who wait.'

'*Pah!*' said Holmes 'Have you ever noticed, Watson, that for every silly aphorism, there's an opposing one. "Those who wait"! What about "The early bird catches the worm"?'

'We might try to catch a bit of the spirit, Holmes. Do you have no childhood Christmas memories?'

'An orange.'

'What?'

'I received an orange at Christmas. And perhaps a book.'

'No special meals? No pine boughs, no singing round a piano?' A sudden image of Holmes and his brother Mycroft as children singing by a piano made me laugh.

'Watson, do pay attention to the task at hand. Much may yet go wrong. There are too many variables.'

'Yes, but again, Holmes? *What* may go wrong? What *are* the variables?'

'Human beings are the variables, Watson. Driven by emotion and always unpredictable. *Aha*, more drinks! Mulled wine, this time.'

A young man served us glasses of the festive drink. We each took one, but Holmes pretended to take a sip then set down that glass on a side table as he had the other. I followed suit and joined him as he moved towards the tall windows that looked out on a row of trees and the carriage-house. I followed his gaze to where several well-dressed coachmen stood huddled around a roaring fire in an outdoor brazier. 'Holmes, do you think the Findlays will try something tonight?'

'It is less likely than before.'

'Why?'

'Because I arranged for them to spend the last five days in a warm hotel. Five days of restful sleep and enough food. And a doctor, someone trained in helping people afflicted like Clarice Findlay.'

'And that was your plan? What possible good could a few days of rest and food do for that unfortunate couple?'

'That is rather the point. Watson. People in their position are undernourished and get little sleep.'

'You could be describing yourself.'

'Watson, do not be specious. Robbery and burglary are common where they live, and life is conducted on the edge of the abyss. Imagine never, even for a moment, feeling safe. The noise, the filth, thieves all around you. One cannot reason, one cannot *think* in such a circumstance.'

'And you suppose that a few days will have given them enough respite . . . to see what is best for their child?' I had heard of doctors helping such as Clarice Findlay, but never in five days. As a doctor I knew that recovery from a laudanum addiction in such short order was wishful thinking.

'Enough food and a good night's sleep can work wonders to increase clarity of thought, Watson.'

I looked around nervously. Gaily dressed children. Doting parents. A sudden childish shriek from the next room startled me, but it was followed by laughter.

'Where are these police, Holmes?'

'Do you see the man with the red mutton-chops, near the opposite window?'

'Yes.'

'Crighton. He is Lestrade's best man. And two more are at this party. The chance of violence is slim. The chance of emotional upheaval, however . . . that is another story.'

'But what if the Findlays try to break in?'

'They will not.'

'How can you be certain?'

'Because they are already here.'

'What? How—?'

Holmes pointed out of the window to one of the drivers. 'See the man in the navy velvet coat?' I squinted through the fading light. The man moved so that the bright fire briefly lit up his face. It was Peter Findlay.

'Hired as an extra groom. And now look into the next room where the food is being laid out.'

I did so and saw three serving maids setting out food. One looked up from her work to glance at someone out of sight. It was Clarice Findlay.

'Good God, Holmes, Mrs Findlay! She is almost a different person.'

And indeed, a remarkable transformation had come over the young woman. Her previously dirty and careworn face was scrubbed and shining, her hair neatly tied back under a lace cap. Even from this distance I could see by her smooth, deft movement as she went about her work that she was not drugged as she had been at her home. Rather, I was struck at the young woman's energy and dexterity as she placed the silver in neat rows for the buffet supper which was to come. And by her beauty. Jonathan's mother was the source of his angelic countenance.

I watched her for a long moment. I wondered at her thoughts, her emotions. If she had been told—and she must have, I reasoned—then she now knew that her own child resided in these rooms, just out of reach.

Seeing the mother in this way brought the pain of her situation to the fore and made me question Holmes's reasoning. While his brilliance at solving crimes was inarguable, he could occasionally be oblivious to human emotion. Could bringing the Findlays here have been a large miscalculation on his part?

Mrs Findlay glanced frequently towards the tree, and as I watched, she edged nearer to the opening between the dining room and the large room in which we now stood.

'Holmes!' I whispered.

'I see her.'

Suddenly she caught sight of Holmes and me, and with a start, she ducked back into the dining room and returned to her task.

'I convinced the Endicotts to hire them as extra hands for this party.'

'Then they know . . . and they agreed? My God, Holmes. The risk!'

'Admittedly there is some, but perhaps less so than otherwise. The Findlays are well aware that they are being watched and that any false move will have serious consequences.'

'But why would the Endicotts agree to this?'

'Watson, they agreed on the condition that you and I be here . . . and the police as well. And that Mr Findlay is not allowed into the house.'

'That did not answer the question.'

'I forced the Endicotts' hand, Watson. I told them the courts might easily award Jonathan to the Findlays should the situation come to trial. The child was taken from them illegally.'

'No! Surely you don't think any judge would—?'

'It is possible, Watson. The verdicts in such cases have been inconsistent. I have done my research. This plan may avert disaster.'

'I don't see how.'

'Watson, nothing is certain. But it is best left in both family's hands.'

'And what *would* be the best in this case, Holmes?'

'That the two sets of parents, together, will come to an accord.'

But the sound of a bell cut him off, and I was left to ponder this conundrum.

Mr and Mrs Endicott appeared from another room with Jonathan between them. The little boy was radiant in a red velvet Christmas suit, lace cuffs, short breeches and shiny shoes. But of course the child was oblivious to all of this as his eyes took in the tree, the gifts and the crowd of children. He smiled and clapped his hands with pleasure.

Lord Endicott tapped a spoon onto a crystal glass and the room quietened.

'Jonathan has a surprise for his fellow children today. In honour of his own birthday, and of Christmas, he would like to give each of you a present,' said he.

Squeals of childish delight pierced the air. Holmes grimaced slightly.

What followed was a theatrical but charming tableau. Lord and Lady Endicott took positions on either side of Jonathan. The gifts were very carefully taken from under the tree, one at a time, by a servant who handed them to the boy. He frowned in concentration at each tag and announced the recipient's name in his soprano voice, impressively able to read at age four.

The child whose name was called would then step forward from amongst the crowd to receive their gift.

At last, three children were left who had not been called, and Lady Endicott asked each of them their names. I saw a footman behind the tree quickly write on a tag and then bring the gift round to the front, as though it had been hidden back there.

In this way, not one child was left out. I was struck by the thoughtfulness of the Endicotts, and in particular the joyful delight Jonathan showed while giving the gifts. I glanced back to the next room where the food had been laid out. Standing in the wide archway which led to this room were twenty or more staff, including Clarice Findlay, watching the entire procedure.

Tears streamed from Mrs Findlay's eyes and she blotted them with her apron.

Behind the serving maids were a number of other servants, including, to my surprise, four grooms, one of whom was Peter Findlay! Now both Findlays were in the house, within sight and reach of the son who had been cruelly stolen from them. I felt a shiver of alarm. Holmes noted Findlay at the same time and frowned in anger. I could only presume it was he who specified that Findlay could not enter the house.

Clarice Findlay leaned forward on her toes, barely able to restrain herself. It seemed she might run precipitously into the room in which we now stood. Findlay quickly moved behind his wife and put his hands on her shoulders. In spite of the man's previous violence, it was Clarice who concerned me more.

I was so distracted by the presence of this dangerous couple,

I nearly missed that Lord Endicott had begun addressing the assembled room. '. . . And it is with great pleasure that we welcome you to share in the bounty that God has bestowed on us here, and join us for a Christmas Eve repast that—'

But Jonathan, at his side, tugged at his father's sleeve.

He looked down at his son and smiled. 'One moment, son,' he said kindly.

'Philip,' said his wife, who waited near the servants at the dining-room entrance. She held up her hands outlining a small box and indicated their little boy. His present! Of course. Jonathan had not yet received *his* gift.

'Oh,' said Lord Endicott. 'Jonathan! We have nearly forgotten your present. *Hmm* . . . let us see then, where could it be?' As he turned towards the dining room the little boy leaned down and peered under the tree. He got down on his hands and knees to see better.

A gasp from the dining room drew my attention. Behind Lady Endicott, a servant appeared. Nestled in his arms was a small, wheat-coloured puppy with an enormous red bow attached to his collar. This, of course, was Jonathan's present! What could be more desired by a child? The servant handed the puppy to Lady Endicott.

I turned back towards the tree to see the little boy's reaction . . . but Jonathan had disappeared. My first thought was . . . the Findlays! But there they were, still in the open doorway to the dining room, along with the other staff. I turned back. Where was the boy? Suddenly there was a slight sway to the tree, and I caught a glimpse of Jonathan's legs underneath it.

'He's under the tree!' one child shouted, laughing.

Next to me Holmes stiffened in alarm.

'Come out from there,' cried Lady Endicott. 'It is dangerous, Jonathan.'

'Listen to your mother,' said Lord Endicott sternly. 'Come out at once!'

The tree swayed slightly.

'Oh, my God, the candles!' said a woman near me.

Several candles had toppled from the upper branches. Up high, a small flame appeared.

A servant was at the tree in an instant with a pail of water that had been positioned nearby, for just such emergencies. Two candles that had fallen were retrieved by another man, but smoke emerged from where the third had ignited a branch. The servant flung the water, and it quickly doused the small flame. What a dangerous and foolish custom. But . . . disaster was averted.

Suddenly a child's cry came from beneath the tree. Perhaps Jonathan had been rained upon by this sudden deluge, I thought. But as we watched in horror, a glow emerged from under the tree.

'Fire!' shouted a man.

Lady Endicott and Clarice Findlay shrieked in unison, and before anyone could stop her, the younger woman broke free from her husband's arms and dashed across the room.

What happened next appeared to me in that moment to be moving slowly, as in a terrible waking dream.

'Christopher!' cried Clarice Findlay. She flung herself to the floor and barrelled clumsily under the tree on her hands and knees, knocking heavily into two branches. More candles fell, some landing on the girl herself. Her skirts ignited, and she screamed.

Several of us leaped towards the tree. But Holmes had beaten us all, thrusting his long, thin frame underneath the branches with the speed of a mongoose snaking up to a cobra. Flames licked the interior of the tree.

'Holmes!'

'More water!' shouted Lord Endicott and servants raced from the room to retrieve it. What had they been thinking? Two pails of water for the entire tree and its many candles!

I heard more shrieks from the crowd. Lady Endicott was restrained by two maids from rushing to the flames.

Holmes had crawled in out of reach, and Clarice flailed in panic, further knocking into the tree as Lord Endicott and I tried to pull her from it. Her skirts aflame, the woman writhed hysterically, sending the entire tree into motion. Another orange flare of fire burst from the branches. We extricated the screaming woman and Peter Findlay tore off his coat and used it to smother the flame on his young wife's skirts as she continued to shriek. Another servant tossed water on the girl.

The tree was now half aflame.

Holmes and the boy had not yet emerged. 'Holmes!' I cried.

Suddenly I heard a strained voice call out. 'I have him! Pull!' It was Holmes. His boots became visible at the edge of the collapsing tree as he attempted to back out from under it.

Lord Endicott and I leaped as one, each grabbed a foot and pulled my friend out from under the tree.

Cradled in his arms was the little boy, protected from the flames by Holmes's own body. The back of my friend's evening jacket was smoking and his left sleeve was afire.

Servants extinguished it in seconds with the water that had been rushed into the room and I took Jonathan from his arms. I looked over the boy quickly. He was white with fear and shaking, but unharmed.

'Mummy!' he whimpered. Lord and Lady Endicott took him from me, and he fell into his mother's arms.

Smoke emanated now from the nearby drapery. 'Everyone out!' cried the butler. I became aware that in the distance, the clang of an approaching fire truck sounded. Holmes staggered to his feet.

A footman and I helped him outside. The snow was welcome after the intense heat we had all just endured.

'I am fine,' he said, shaking us off.

Nevertheless, I sat him on a stone bench and rubbed wet snow on the sleeve that had caught fire. It had burned clean away, but I could not see the damage due to the blackened shirtsleeve beneath it. Firemen raced past us into the house.

Holmes looked up at me. 'The boy?'

'Jonathan is fine,' I said. 'Not a hair was harmed. Thanks to you.'

Holmes closed his eyes and smiled.

'But you,' I said, 'need a doctor. Fortunately one is here. Bring scissors,' I commanded a nearby servant.

# CHAPTER 19

## The Christmas Angel

Christmas angel must have been in attendance at the Endicotts' party because while the room suffered damage, no one was seriously injured. I quickly attended to Holmes, who was affected far less than the sleeve of his finest frock coat. Dr Anthony Hughes, the Endicotts' Harley Street family physician, came forth and attended to Mrs Findlay, who was more frightened than hurt.

Some thirty minutes later, the house cleared of guests and the fire safely out, Holmes demanded a meeting with both sets of parents. Lord Endicott, the Findlays, Holmes and I gathered in Lady Endicott's salon, where she had received us last week. I perched nervously on a velvet chair, uneasy at what was to come. I fingered the Webley in my jacket pocket, keeping a wary eye on the violent Mr Findlay, but he sat calmly with his arm around his young wife, who dabbed at her streaming eyes. Lestrade's men waited, respectful but alert, in the open doorway.

Anything, I thought, could happen next.

Holmes stood in front of the darkened window, through which a persistent snowfall glimmered in the light from outdoor lanterns. He was on edge. I had no idea what to expect from the gathering, and from his own drawn look it seemed that he was not sure, either.

Lord Endicott stood near the fireplace, seething. 'Why do you insist on this pointless meeting?' he demanded of Holmes. 'Surely your plan for this evening did not include this disaster?'

'Of course not.'

'Now that the story is in the open, these people can see that the child is suitably housed. I shall sue for permanent custody and we will easily get it,' said Endicott.

'I must advise caution, Lord Endicott,' said Holmes. 'There are precedents in both directions. It is entirely unclear who would win custody. It would be best for the child—and indeed this was my plan here—if the four of you came to an accord privately.'

'Imagine the damage to Jonathan if you took this case to trial,' I added.

'*Christopher*,' said Peter Findlay, quietly.

A taut silence pervaded the room. The fire crackling blended into the soft sound of some carollers down the street.

The maid, Jenny, and Hector the bodyguard entered with

200

Jonathan, who cradled his new puppy in his arms. The boy ran to Lady Endicott. 'Mummy, I love my doggie! Can he sleep with me?' he cried, kissing the puppy's head. The dog responded by licking the boy's face.

Lady Endicott embraced the child and patted the dog. 'Not in your bed, darling. I think he has his own little basket nearby?' The maid nodded. 'Time for sleep now, dear one,' said she. 'Enough excitement for the day.'

'I was scared, Papa,' said Jonathan to Lord Endicott.

'Foolish of you to go under the tree, young man,' said Endicott, tousling the boy's hair. 'You must always look before you leap.'

I glanced at the Findlays, who sat motionless, watching this intently.

'Thank Mr Holmes here,' said Lady Endicott to the boy. 'He saved you.'

Clarice Findlay made a small whimpering sound.

'My wife tried, as well,' said Findlay.

'Thank you,' said the child, looking from Holmes to Clarice Findlay and back. He approached my friend. 'Would you like to pet him?' he asked, holding out the puppy with a smile. Holmes nodded and scratched behind the animal's ears.

The boy then approached Clarice Findlay. 'What is your name?' he asked with the special gravitas of the very young.

'I . . . I . . . Clarice. I am . . .'

'Thank you for trying to save me, Mrs Clarice,' said the little boy. 'It was very brave of you. What do you think of my puppy?'

201

Clarice paused, trembling. She reached out a hand and patted the dog awkwardly. 'He . . . he is gold. He—'

'Goldie!' cried the boy. 'That's his name! Goldie!'

Clarice stared at the boy and smiled shyly.

'Mummy!' squealed the boy. Clarice started, but now the boy had turned to Lady Endicott and raced back to her, leaning into her gentle embrace. 'Mummy!' he said. 'His name is Goldie! The bestest name! The bestest doggie. Don't you think so, Mummy?'

Clarice watched this in silence. A tear spilled down her face.

'I think it is a splendid name, Jonathan. And now, off to bed,' said Lady Endicott.

The boy secured a brief hug from Lord Endicott and was led from the room.

Findlay remained stoic, but his wife buried her head into her husband's shoulder and softly wept.

'Never candles on the tree, never again,' Lady Endicott said.

'It was a danger to everyone,' said Peter Findlay.

'It is time to get to heart of the matter,' said Holmes. 'I would like to conduct this next business in private. Are we safe to do so, Mr Findlay?' He gestured towards the police, still standing watch in the doorway.

Findlay nodded, ashamed.

Lord Endicott stood up and closed the doors on the police with a pointed look at Findlay. He returned to his wife's side.

Holmes stood and cleared his throat. 'We begin. There

are a number of points to resolve. Lord and Lady Endicott, as I told you, your Jonathan was born Christopher Findlay, to Mr and Mrs Findlay here, while they were residents of the Marylebone Workhouse. He was taken by the matron there, Mrs Claudia Huron, and given to the Bright Little Ones adoption agency, where you adopted him.'

'We were told he was an orphan,' said Lord Endicott. 'You know that.'

'That is what Mrs Huron told the agency,' said Holmes.

'We would never have stolen someone else's child,' whispered Lady Endicott.

'Understood,' said Holmes. He turned to the other couple. 'Mr and Mrs Findlay, the Endicotts adopted the baby boy in good faith. Aside from wealth, the child has been showered with love.' He turned back to the Endicotts. 'But, Lord and Lady Endicott, the Findlays *are* Jonathan's birth parents.'

'Christopher! He's mine!' cried Clarice Findlay. 'And I want him back! Shouldn't I?' All eyes turned to her. In her wide-eyed desperation, her extreme youth was evident. She looked barely out of her teens.

Clarice Findlay looked at each person in the room, wanting an answer. No one replied. 'Mine,' whimpered Clarice. She looked up at her husband. 'Peter?'

He looked sadly down at his wife.

'I will be a good girl, Peter. I will be a good girl! A good mum!'

Peter Findlay swallowed and said nothing.

203

'Mr Findlay,' said Holmes, 'tell the Endicotts what made you suddenly believe your child was alive, and that he was here?'

Findlay took a deep breath and stood up, next to his wife. Endicott stiffened, on the alert. But Findlay only put a comforting hand on his wife's shoulder.

'I . . . read about Mrs Huron's trial in the newspaper. The false adoptions. Mrs Huron, that woman! It was she who found Christopher dead, or so she told us. I believed her. But now I thought, what if he hadn't died and she'd taken him, too?'

'You then went to the two adoption agencies mentioned in the article to inquire about the child,' said Holmes. 'The first was closed, and then you were rebuffed at Bright Little Ones. You returned and ransacked the office, finding the records that proved your child—with his distinctive port-wine stain—had lived and was adopted by the Endicotts. What did you do next?'

'I wrote to Lord Endicott!' He turned to face Endicott. 'Yes, I wrote to you, sir. Twice.'

'Philip?' Lady Endicott turned to her husband in astonishment. 'Those two letters you burned?'

'Extortion, I thought,' said Endicott. 'A man in my position is frequently approached.'

'I wrote to you in good faith. You could have responded,' said Findlay.

Endicott said nothing.

'Why, then, did you not pursue legal means to regain your son, Mr Findlay?' I asked.

'I tried,' said the man gravely. 'Rudyard Click would not take our case.'

'Why not?'

Findlay looked at his feet. This next was difficult for him. 'He said . . . he said he smelled drink on me. And Mrs Huron had told him some things—'

'Who the bloody hell is Rudyard Click?' said Lord Endicott.

'Click was the solicitor who presented the case against Mrs Huron and sent her to prison,' said Holmes. 'Two falsely adopted children have all been restored to their birth parents. You would be wise to pay careful attention, Lord Endicott.' He turned back to Findlay. 'You all know what transpired next. Mr Findlay, recount it please.'

Peter Findlay took a deep breath and nodded. Turning to Lord Endicott, he said, 'Sir, abject apologies to you for breaking into your home, terrifying the servants and guests, like some kind of common criminal.' He turned to Lady Endicott. 'And even deeper apologies to you, madam, for my terrible actions on Oxford Street. I never meant for you to fall. It was an accident.' A tear appeared on his cheek and he wiped it away. 'But . . . but I was doing it for the good of—'

'You can't tell me you were doing it for the boy!' cried Lord Endicott. 'Imagine his terror, being wrenched from his bed or from his mother's arms by a violent stranger? What kind of home could *you* provide him? No judge in the world would—'

'Let Mr Findlay continue,' said Holmes. 'Gentlemen, sit down, please.'

Findlay did so, and his wife buried her face in his shoulder.

Endicott sat next to his wife with reluctance, still fuming.

Findlay took a deep breath and continued. 'When I tried to abduct our son, I will be honest. I wasn't—'

'Twice! You tried twice!' Lord Endicott cried, rising to his feet.

'Philip,' said Lady Endicott, laying a hand on his arm. 'Calm yourself. I know how much you love our child. But do sit down.'

Endicott paused, then resumed his seat.

'I . . . I will admit, I wasn't doing it for the boy,' said Peter Findlay. 'I was doing it for Clarice.' He drew her closer. 'Everything I have done, I have done for her. And I am so very sorry.'

The room went silent. A log turned in the fireplace and crumbled in a shower of sparks. Both couples started.

Findlay swallowed, paused, cleared his throat. 'Mrs Huron took our son for a reason. Four days before . . . before he left us, Clarice took a baby soother intended for the child and thus under the spell of laudanum, fell asleep. She left our Christopher—that is the name we gave him— on the cold stone floor of her cell, where he nearly froze to death. He was three weeks old. I found the boy just in time and rescued him. So when Mrs Huron told me she had found him there a second time, and this time too late, I . . . had no reason to doubt it.'

Clarice stared vacantly into space as her husband continued his story.

'Clarice was never the same after that, thinking she had caused our son's death.'

Endicott said, more calmly, 'Well, even tonight, this careless woman—'

'Lord Endicott,' I interrupted. 'Mrs Findlay bravely dived into danger to save the child.' As much as I wanted the child to stay with the Endicotts, the man was being cruelly unfair.

'My wife did do that!' said Findlay. He hugged his wife closer. 'You were very brave, darling.'

'Yes, she was,' said Holmes. 'Mr Findlay, continue, please.'

Turning back to the Endicotts, Findlay said, 'You see a criminal before you, sir, and that is *all* you see. But it is not all that I am. I am an educated man, a trained maritime engineer, driven to desperate measures. You, sir, with all your privileges, have no idea how a decent man can descend overnight into poverty. You cannot imagine the effects of this life.'

Endicott made to reply but his wife put her hand on his arm.

Findlay continued. 'Four and a half years ago I lost my job when the company for whom I worked was sold. I then fell ill for a month with fever. Just as I recovered, our neighbours in the building fell asleep with a pot on the fire, and the only home we knew burned to the ground, along with everything we owned. We were destitute. Winter was coming on, and my Clarice was with child. Our choice was the workhouse or to die of the cold.'

I glanced at the Endicotts. They listened intently.

'Once there,' Findlay continued, 'I fell into despair and, for the first time in my life, I am ashamed to admit . . . I took to drink.' His face clouded and he looked down at the floor. 'I now know, sir, that I am a man who should never raise a glass again. And I will not.'

Findley continued. 'Only Mrs Huron saw any good in me at that awful place and allowed me familial visits with Clarice up to and after Christopher's birth. But after . . . after Christopher's death, or so I thought, I got another job, found a home for the two of us, and thought us to be on the mend. But Clarice was inconsolable. Nothing seemed to bring her back to herself.'

'Poor girl,' said Lady Endicott. 'But Mr Findlay, perhaps a doctor—an alienist—could help your wife?'

'Perhaps, madam. Clarice was but fifteen at Christopher's birth,' said Findlay. 'Laudanum took her in its grip and has her still. I tried to make things right by setting her up in business—a baby minding service for the factory girls. I thought that caring for infants would bring her back.'

'But you were wrong, Mr Findlay,' said Holmes. 'Your wife's addiction has impaired her judgment. And she has been drugging her charges.'

A sharp intake of breath from Lady Endicott.

'No . . .' moaned the girl, still buried into her husband's shoulder.

Peter Findlay loosened her grip and stroked his wife's forehead. 'You were, Clarice.'

'I love my son,' said Clarice defensively. 'I love Christopher.'

'Mr Findlay, I have a question for you,' said Holmes. 'It

could not have been a complete surprise to you that your poor wife was unsuitable for the business you set up for her. She is still in need of help, even now. It will take much more than my short intervention to remedy this situation.'

'Explain yourself, Mr Holmes.' Lady Endicott said, staring at Holmes.

'I provided for the Findlays five days of rest, in a safe, quiet place, Lady Endicott. Five days of good, nutritious meals and medical care,' said Holmes. 'That has effected the transformation you see in Mr Findlay. It is remarkable what a sound body can do for sound thinking. But *only if the mind is capable of logic.* My hope lies with you, Mr Findlay, to see and do the right thing.'

'It was an accident, tonight! Not my fault!' cried Clarice Findlay.

'Hush, darling,' said Findlay. 'Not your fault at all. You tried to save the child.' He looked up at my friend. 'Mr Holmes, your plan worked. I have seen the grotesque error I have made. And I am ready to make the right decision, both for my Clarice and for our son.'

Endicott stood, ready to assert sovereignty, but his wife pulled him back next to her.

The girl looked up at her husband. 'Peter?'

'Darling, we must leave Christopher with parents who love him and who can give him the best possible life,' he said.

'But he's ours!' she cried.

'Clarice, my love, consider this,' said Findlay. 'Christopher believes them to be his parents and he is happy. Can you see what he has here? It is far more than money, my darling.'

Clarice gasped and stared at her husband.

'It would break his heart to take him away from all that he has known,' said he.

My God, Holmes was right again. He had seen the rational and loving man behind Peter Findlay's apparent criminality. A man no one else, including me, had discerned. 'What, then, is your plan, Findlay?' asked Holmes.

'I have been offered a position in Liverpool. We will move north and begin again.'

'You are still young,' I said.

Findlay nodded. He turned to his wife. 'Clarice. All will be well. You see what Christopher has here. What he is now accustomed to. Mr Holmes is right. This is best for all.'

'But I can get better,' she whined. 'I can be a good girl.'

He put his arm around her. 'I believe you can be . . . a very good girl. And now, let us give our son the best gift of all. Give him . . . all of this. It is in your power, my darling.'

Endicott could barely restrain himself, but his wise wife put her hand on his arm.

Clarice paused. She looked around at the beautiful room, then at the elegant couple who clearly loved the boy. I glanced at Holmes. His face gave nothing away.

'Let me take care of you,' said Findlay to his wife. 'We shall begin again. What do you say, my darling?'

Clarice hiccoughed and wiped tears away. 'All right,

Peter,' she said at last. 'All right. Christopher should . . .
He should stay.'

At the portico, as the Findlays prepared to depart in a
carriage provided for them by the Endicotts, Lady Endicott
took Clarice Findlay by the hands. 'Thank you, Mrs Findlay.
Jonathan . . . Christopher . . . will be cherished.'

Clarice Findlay looked up at Lady Endicott, then at Lord
Endicott beside her. Her voice was barely a whisper. 'Love
him for me. Love him . . . so much . . .'

Lady Endicott nodded, and her own tears matched
Clarice's. 'I will write to you every year at Christmas. You
will know what becomes of him.'

'Thank you.'

Findlay helped his wife into the carriage. He started to
follow. Holmes put a hand out to stop him. 'Not yet. There
is still business to conclude,' he prompted. 'Mr Findlay,
make your pledge.'

Findlay turned to Lord Endicott and steeled himself. 'I
will sign all papers, granting you full custody. The falsely
documented adoption will never come to trial,' said Findlay.

Lady Endicott exhaled in relief, and Lord Endicott nodded.

'Lord Endicott, it is to you,' Holmes prompted.

Lord Endicott put his arm around his wife. 'I will not
file charges against you, Mr Findlay. But . . . never set foot
near us again.'

'Agreed,' said Findlay.

'Excellent. Consider it the greatest Christmas gift that
you give each other,' said Holmes. 'And to your son.'

The coach departed. We watched it proceed down the street, passing some carollers along the way. One of the Endicotts' footmen whistled to a passing cab. Holmes broke the spell.

'No cab, thank you, I should like to walk. But Dr Watson's wife would dearly love his presence at least for the remainder of this evening. And there is a roast goose awaiting you, is there not, Doctor?'

'If there is any left,' I said. 'But I shall walk back to Baker Street with you.' As we set out, I felt a rush of relief for the boy, happiness for Lord and Lady Endicott . . . and dare I say it, hope for Mr Findlay and his poor, childlike wife.

# CHAPTER 20

## *Wrapped and Delivered*

s the light snow fell softly around us, we strolled northward to Baker Street in silence, past elegant homes which soon gave way to a more commercial area. We passed the windows of shuttered shops, finding our images eerily reflected in their darkened glass panes.

Near Green Street, the sudden bang of a window drew my attention up to a young man who leaned out from a first floor, lighting up a cigar, the sound of laughter spilling out around him. A young woman in a red dress appeared behind him, removed the cigar from his mouth and—holding some mistletoe above their heads—kissed him. I laughed, thinking of the welcome I'd be given by my own wife within the next hour or so.

But once back in Baker Street, I was loath to abandon

Holmes without at least a celebratory drink. As I unwound the scarf from my neck and entered the sitting-room, I was surprised to find Heffie there, seated and reading from a small book. On her lap was another, larger book, and Christmas wrapping paper was strewn about her stockinged feet.

'Heffie,' said Holmes. 'I was not expecting you tonight. I see you found your gifts.'

'This book is really a strange 'un, Mr 'olmes,' said she, holding up the smaller of the two. '*Flatland*. There's no people! Only . . . shapes and lines and things.'

'Yes.'

I had heard of that book. Something to do with mathematics.

'And this other 'un. *Origin of the Species*. Idea seems interestin'. I usually reads novels, though lately I find 'em borin'.'

'I thought a little science and mathematics were due to you,' said Holmes.

Again, the 'improving' gift. I laughed.

'What 'appened to you there?' asked Heffie. Holmes had removed his frock coat and was rolling up his burnt sleeve, revealing beneath it my impromptu bandage.

'Nothing. Just a little fire. Watson, pour us a whisky, would you?' said my friend. 'Then, really, you must both be off. I insist.' He moved off into his bedroom.

'Heffie, a whisky for you, too?' I asked.

'A quick 'un!' said the girl, as she pulled her discarded boots towards her. Holmes returned, having donned his purple dressing-gown.

'You sound like me mum, Mr 'olmes. She were on about my learnin', too. She were so smart.'

Holmes sighed. 'You understate. Did you know, Heffie, that at the time of her death, she was in line to be the headmistress at the school where she taught?'

Heffie was caught by surprise at this and for a brief second I thought that I saw tears, although perhaps it was a trick of the firelight. 'No,' said she. 'I . . . I did not know that.'

'Your mother was exceptional,' continued Holmes. 'As was your father, no doubt.'

''E couldn't string six words together!' said Heffie. 'But why're you investigatin' me?'

'Heffie, your father was a boxer. Head injuries can diminish a man,' said he. 'Your mother would not have married a fool.'

Heffie shrugged, put her boots on and leaned down to fasten them.

I poured whisky into three glasses, thinking that the perils of boxing were precisely why I'd repeatedly implored Holmes to give up the brutal sport. Did he listen? I doubted it.

'But Mr 'olmes, you ain't answered the question,' said Heffie.

'I ain't?' said Holmes with a smile.

'All right, you *haven't*,' said she. 'Why're you—?'

'To know you. Heffie, are you a proponent of Locke's *tabula rasa* or the theory of hereditary traits, as espoused by Darwin?'

'I ain—I *haven't* any idea what you're talking about.'

'Read that book and you shall. I am of the opinion that both heredity and circumstance play roles in shaping a man. My theory is that you have inherited a great deal more intelligence than you credit yourself, and it would be a terrible shame for you not to put it to use.'

Heffie, clearly uncomfortable, took her whisky from me, and downed it in a single gulp.

'P'raps so, Mr 'olmes. I'll give these a look. Now, I'm off! Oh, and I brung you a present, too.' From her voluminous coat pockets, she pulled out two papayas and set them on the sideboard. 'From my new friends in Covent Garden. Merry Christmas!' she called and departed into the night.

I handed Holmes his glass. The whisky glinted topaz in the firelight, and he regarded it solemnly.

'Holmes, before I go?'

'Yes, Watson.'

'Regarding heredity, do think it possible that Jonathan might grow into the violence and dissipation of his birth father, Peter Findlay?'

'I am surprised at this question, Watson. Did you not just witness the poor man finding the best of himself before our very eyes this evening?'

'It was a remarkable transformation, I will admit. How on earth did you predict that a few days of comfort would effect such a change?'

'Observation, Watson. His intelligence, his will, his regard for his wife, perhaps. I caught a glimpse on Oxford Street

216

of his horror at having knocked Lady Endicott to the ground. It was at that moment that I was able to wrest the child away.'

'Well, that is something.'

'Consider this. Poverty and ill luck can bring down the strongest of men. The poorest in this city are so constrained by their circumstances that, no matter what their gifts or innate proclivities, it is hard to rise above the morass in which they are trapped.'

'I suppose.'

'They are rather like the prehistoric animals mired in tar. Even the mighty mastodon could not pull free. The sabre-toothed tiger, entrapped next to the gazelle. Strong and weak flail about, both trapped in their circumstance. And in an effort to escape, nearby creatures are accidental casualties.'

The metaphor seemed fantastical, but I supposed it made sense. 'Poor Clarice,' I said.

Holmes nodded. 'What forges some, melts others. He may save her yet.' He held out his glass. 'But let us toast now two fathers who thought they knew best for their sons,' said he.

'To little Jonathan Endicott and his bright future.' I said, raising my glass.

'And to Katarina Descanso and George Perkins,' added Holmes. We drank.

'When, exactly did you know that Katarina was Reginald, Holmes?'

'I suspected immediately, of course But I was not perfectly

certain until the moment I felt the faintest hint of stubble. Where are my slippers?'

'Under that chair,' I said. 'I recall that Irene Adler would occasionally amuse herself dressed as a man.'

Holmes waved his hand dismissively, as if willing the memory away. He retrieved his slippers and put them on.

'Miss Odelia Wyndham, as well,' said I, remembering the unfortunate young lady in a case I'd documented earlier as *The Three Locks*.

'True. But in those cases, both women amused themselves with the added freedom of their male personae. Reginald Weathering . . . Katarina . . . is quite different from these, Watson.'

I nodded. 'I cannot argue. A second toast, then, to your Christmas triumph, Holmes. Two missing sons, now found.' We downed our drinks and at last I picked up my scarf from where I'd thrown it on a chair and wrapped it around my neck.

Holmes took up a strangely shaped package from the sideboard and handed it to me. 'One more little miracle, Watson. Before you go, here is a gift for Mary. But first, you must guess what it is.'

I took the package and felt its shape. It was odd and heavy. It felt like a metal container, in some kind of elaborate design with many sharp corners.

Holmes smiled at my puzzlement. 'Observe and deduce, Watson.'

'No idea, Holmes. A footbath for a pelican, perhaps?'

Holmes laughed. 'The label, Watson, do be thorough,' said he.

I examined the label. '*From the Atelier of Mrs Agnes Marshall, Charlotte Street, Fitzrovia.*' This meant nothing to me. 'Who is Mrs Agnes Marshall?'

'Have you not heard of Mrs Marshall's famous cooking school?'

'No.'

'Your wife, no doubt, knows of her. Mrs Marshall is renowned as a chef, teacher, cookery book author and entrepreneur. Her school in Fitzrovia attracts the very best chefs and even their wealthy female employers. Her indispensable *Book of Cookery* no doubt rests in the kitchen of your own home.'

'I see. But what is this thing, Holmes?'

He hooted with laughter. 'Mrs Marshall is famous for her iced desserts, and this is a mould for a star-shaped version. But more importantly, why do you suppose I made my way to Mrs Marshall's atelier?' My friend now reclined on the sofa, the picture of comfort in his dressing-gown and slippers.

'You confound me, Holmes.' Few people were less interested in cooking than he.

'Remember Felicity, the orphan that Mrs Turner at Bright Little Ones offered to me as a cook and, quite frankly, concubine? Well, Mycroft did my bidding and—'

'Mycroft *did your bidding*?'

'*Ha!* It happens occasionally, Watson, although the debt weighs heavily. In any case, he went to Mrs Turner and was similarly offered the girl. He "purchased" Felicity, then promptly shut down Bright Little Ones. The other children offered by them are being taken in by a reputable orphanage.'

'Excellent!'

'He then secured for Felicity an apprenticeship in Mrs Marshall's school, a position which includes room, board and a salary, and ensures a future for the girl as a well-paid cook.'

'Marvellous, Holmes! You have truly embodied the spirit of Christmas! Now, one last attempt. Will you not change your mind and come home with me to join us for dinner?'

But I already knew the answer. The dressing-gown, the slippers . . . He would be going nowhere.

Holmes reached for his violin. 'Watson, music will be my companion this evening. Be off now. And Merry Christmas, dear friend.'

He put the violin to his chin, and with an impish smile began to saw away merrily at 'God Rest Ye Merry Gentlemen'. The happy tune echoed down the stairs as I descended and came to a rousing finish just as I closed the door behind me. What a triumph he had wrought. I was exhilarated to have been a part of it.

As I stood in the snowy silence in front of 221B, I could see Holmes silhouetted in the window as he drew the violin to his chin once more. A poignant melody in a minor key rang out over the deserted, snow-covered street. A tune from my childhood. What was it?

I stood staring up at him for a long moment. The silvery notes floated down, familiar and haunting, as the tune emerged from the fog of memory into clarity. It was

'Greensleeves'. Or, as reimagined for Christmas, 'What Child is This?'

My friend Sherlock Holmes, who professed to hate the holidays, perhaps embodied the spirit of Christmas more than any man I knew. I smiled all the way home to Mary.

For interesting facts and pictures pertaining to the people
and places in this book, please visit the author's website

www.macbird.com

and particularly this page:

https://macbird.com/what-child-is-this/notes

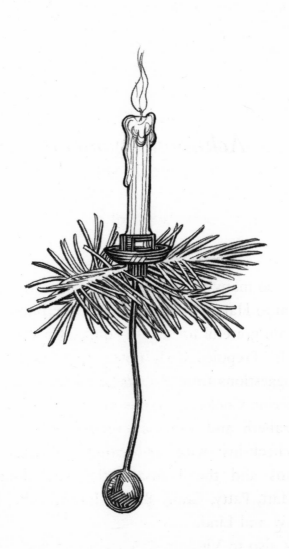

# Acknowledgements

As always, so many people deserve a tip of the deerstalker. In addition to HarperCollins' long-serving publisher David Brawn, I am grateful for astute input from Dana Isaacson and Charles Prepolec, early notes from Lynn Hightower, careful suggestions from Robert Mammana, Alex Bennett and Catherine Cooke, generous and sensitive analyses by Lynn Elizabeth and Vanessa Freudenberg, and ongoing weekly check-ins with crit-group colleagues in the Oxnardians and the Transatlantics, including Miguel, Harley, Matt, Patty, Craig, Bryan, Jamie, Luke, Kateland, JB, Andrew and Linda.

Thanks also to Vincent W. Wright and Richard Burnip, and for moral and other support to Ross Davies, Dennis Palumbo, Gayle Goddard, Rosa Glenn Reilly, Tony Hughes, David Reuben, Don Lawrence, Jonathan LeBillon, Miranda Andrews, Christine Sofiane, Ryan Johnson, Dora Montes,

Freya Shih, Julie McKuras and Linda Langton. Loving thanks and a hug to Nina You.

Frank Cho thrilled me with his willingness to illustrate; his genius is evident and I am so grateful.

It was a particularly tough year and I especially want to express my love and gratitude to my husband, Alan Kay, who bravely travelled through hell during the writing of this book. Alan's stoicism, courage and insistence that I prioritize my work during this year of deep challenges lit up the way for me to carry on through some very dark days. I am so blessed. Thank you, Alan.

Thank you all.

# About the Author

Born in San Francisco, Bonnie MacBird lives in Los Angeles and London, just off Baker Street. She has degrees in music and film from Stanford and has been a passionate Holmes fan since the age of ten. Prior to writing novels, she spent thirty years in Hollywood as a development executive, screenwriter (original writer of *TRON*), Emmy winning producer, and actor.

MacBird is a Baker Street Irregular, on the Council of the Sherlock Holmes Society of London, and a member of many Sherlockian scions. Her first Holmes novel *Art in the Blood* was translated into seventeen languages and began her series, of which this novel is the fifth. They can be read in any order, and the author invites readers to check out her online annotations for a deeper dive into the facts behind the stories.

Visit her at www.macbird.com.

# About the Artist

Frank Cho was born near Seoul, South Korea, in 1971, and his family moved to Maryland in the United States when he was six. He never had any formal training in art but taught himself to write and draw by reading art books and comics. He launched the comic strip *Liberty Meadows* in 1997 and was later recruited by Marvel Entertainment. He has worked on many top-tier books at Marvel, including *Spider-Man*, *The Mighty Avengers*, *Hulk*, *X-Men*, *Shanna the She-Devil* and *Savage Wolverine*. Most recently Frank has received acclaim for his *Harley Quinn* covers for DC. He also works on his creator-owned projects, such as *Fight Girls*, *Skyborne* and *World of Payne* with famed novelist Thomas Sniegoski. A longtime fan of Sherlock Holmes, Frank is also a member of the Baker Street Irregulars.